MIRANDA REWRITTEN

Durango Street Theatre – Book 7

Emily Mims

ALSO BY EMILY MIMS

Durango Street Theatre

Vivi's Leading Man

Maggie's Starring Role

Wade's Dangerous Debut

Jessica's Hero

Letti's Second Act

Cameron Unscripted

The Smoky Blues series

Mist

Smoke

Evergreen

Indigo

Emerald

Mistletoe

Violet

Ruby

Amethyst

Noelle

The Texas Hill Country series

Solomon's Choice

After the Heartbreak

A Gift of Trust

Daughter of Valor

Welcome Home

Unexpected Assets

Never and Always

A Gift of Hope

Once, Again

Other Romances

Season of Enchantment

A Dangerous Attraction

For the Thrill of It All

www.BOROUGHSPUBLISHINGGROUP.com

PUBLISHER'S NOTE: This is a work of fiction. Names, characters, places and incidents either are the product of the author's imagination or are used fictitiously. Any resemblance to actual events, locales, business establishments or persons, living or dead, is coincidental. Boroughs Publishing Group does not have any control over and does not assume responsibility for author or third-party websites, blogs or critiques or their content.

MIRANDA REWRITTEN
Copyright © 2021 Emily Wright Mims

All rights reserved. Unless specifically noted, no part of this publication may be reproduced, scanned, stored in a retrieval system or transmitted in any form or by any means, electronic, mechanical, photocopying, recording, or otherwise, known or hereinafter invented, without the express written permission of Boroughs Publishing Group. The scanning, uploading and distribution of this book via the Internet or by any other means without the permission of Boroughs Publishing Group is illegal and punishable by law. Participation in the piracy of copyrighted materials violates the author's rights.

ISBN 978-1-953810- 65-6

To every man and woman who has had the courage to face their demons and embark on their own Twelve Step journey. God bless you all.

ACKNOWLEDGMENTS

As always, I did not write this book in a vacuum. I want to thank my beta readers Roy Bartels and Edwin Floyd for their insight and suggestions.

Michelle, thank you so much for another awesome edit, and thank you to the Boroughs Art Department for putting the perfect Miranda on the cover.

Thank you, thank you, thank you to real-life Production Manager Denise Ebarra for a look into her world. Thanks as well to the rest of the folks at the Woodlawn Theatre. I love you all!

SENSITIVITY NOTE

This story deals with real life traumas, and focuses on alcoholism, adultery, the loss of a child to cancer, and the loss of a spouse to a horrible car accident. The repercussions of alcoholism are not sugarcoated, and the after-effects of loss is shown for what it is – devasting.

MIRANDA REWRITTEN

Chapter One

Miranda

The night Miranda's best friend died in a car accident she hadn't been heading home from the Durango Street Theatre as everyone had presumed. Nope. She'd just climbed out of Miranda's brother's bed. Renee had been at it with Butch for about six months, this the most recent in a long line of affairs over the last ten years of her life. Miranda had never breathed a word to anybody. Especially not the cops at the accident scene.

As she stared from mid-orchestra at Renee's daughter, Emma—who's first song was coming up soon in the Durango's post-Covid debut production of *West Side Story*—Miranda knew she'd never told the authorities the truth of Renee's whereabouts because of Emma. At the time, the girl was too young to have comprehended the implications, but when she got older, the whispers would haunt her.

Emma had become the daughter of Miranda's heart, and she happily played guardian angel in all sorts of ways. Like helping get Emma away from her drunk, abusive, asshole of a father, Ross Ellis. Two years ago, Emma had moved in with her maternal grandparents, and it didn't take long before she blossomed. Like most kids in the country, she'd finished high school remotely, and was starting her freshman year at a local small college this fall. Leaving her father's house and moving in with the Summersets was the best thing that could've happened to her. It was what Renee would've wanted for her daughter.

Clipboard in hand, Miranda stood beside the light and sound board for a few minutes watching the beginning of the "Dance at the Gym" ballet sequence between the Sharks and the Jets. Years ago, she'd given up her job in a small-town beauty salon and gone to work for the Durango as their full-time production manager. She still did a lot of the hairstyles and wigs for the theater, but these days, those were only a small part of her job. Managing the productions consumed most of her time and energy.

Since things seemed to be running smoothly, Miranda decided to continue her supervision from her favorite hidey-hole. She ducked into the lobby and moved aside the stand with the velvet ropes and climbed the steep, carpeted stairs to the freshly cleaned balcony, empty except for the musical director and the orchestra members cloistered in the small individual rooms in the sound booth.

Looking around, she saw the balcony wasn't truly empty. A lone figure sat in the back row with a ballcap pulled low over his? face. Whoever it was appeared to be watching the stage intently. Miranda wondered why they chose to sit in the back row of the balcony rather than in their purchased seat downstairs. Well, whoever it was, they weren't hurting anyone. If they were still up here later, she would make it a point to find out what was going on.

When Emma's first song began, Miranda watched with pride as the girl took her place on the stage as Rosalia and sang the newcomer's sarcastic take on American life.

Emma recently graduated from the Academy and was the youngest member of the cast. Miranda was the one who'd reached out to the lonely girl who was mired in grief and trapped in a house with her alcoholic father. She'd enlisted the help of Renee's influential parents, and the Summersets had overridden Ross's objections and had assured Emma's continued involvement in the Academy.

Miranda's involvement in Emma's life went far beyond the theater, and in some ways the relationship eased the pain of her own son's untimely death. Emma and Tommy had gone to nursery school together and had been in the same grade in elementary school. The young girl had been there for her son while he fought for his life and lost, and she'd laid a bouquet of sunflowers on his casket before they lowered him into the ground.

She'd laid sunflowers on her mother's casket eight years later.

Miranda made herself shake off the heartrending memories. Tonight was a night for joy, pride, and new beginnings. Emma was rockin' the stage, and Miranda couldn't have been prouder. The story moved along and she continued taking notes on what was working and what needed attention, and before she knew it, Tony and Maria were singing "One Hand, One Heart."

It was time to go downstairs.

She got up and saw the mysterious figure was still sitting motionless in the back row, looking down at what seemed to be a program. *Good luck with reading in the dark.*

She made a couple of notes and went downstairs as the house lights came on and patrons flooded the lobby, lined up at the restrooms, and waited for a treat at the concession stand.

Fifteen minutes later, when the lights dimmed, Miranda went back to the balcony. As she climbed the steps, she wondered if the mysterious figure was still there and sure enough, the person was sitting motionless in the top row. Now she was really curious.

She continued to make notes as the story came to the inevitable, heartbreaking conclusion. Swallowing the ridiculous lump in her throat, through her tiny mic she ordered the curtain closed, and then open again as the actors came out to take their bows.

As the performers curtsied and bowed, applause began to echo around the auditorium. The house lights winked on slowly and the figure in the ballcap raised his head and skewered her with a piercing glare. She froze on the steps as she stared into blue eyes burning into hers with disdain. *Ross Ellis.* Emma's drunken bastard of a father, and owner of the Red Rock Ranch. Miranda's neighbor one farm over. The man who'd neglected her best friend for years and had gotten thrown out of the theater when he'd terrified his daughter.

What the hell was he doing at the Durango?

They stared at one another for a moment as Miranda's shock slowly morphed into the contempt remembering his drunken scene during *Shrek* rehearsals when he'd terrorized a rehearsal room of teenage girls, and had mortified his daughter.

It'd taken weeks before Emma felt comfortable returning to the theater, and even two years later, it had taken every bit of Miranda's persuasive power to convince Emma to audition for *West Side Story.*

Not that Ross had been around for any more drunken tirades. He'd disappeared less than a week after being chucked onto the sidewalk.

The pitiful remnants of a once profitable herd of cattle had been sold off at auction, and his fields were lying fallow. He hadn't been seen anywhere, and gossip had flown in the small farming community of Pleasanton as to where he was, what he was doing, and if he was even alive.

Miranda hadn't known, and she sure as hell hadn't given a damn. He was out of his daughter's life, and it was all that mattered.

Now the bastard was back. Her gaze flicked over him as he unfolded his considerable height from the chair, his eyes still fixed on her and his expression clearly hostile. She took in his appearance. He'd once been a handsome man with firm, even features, dimples in his cheeks and a ready smile. Once upon a time, she'd been attracted to him. Now he looked older than his forty-two years, with deep grooves running across his forehead and bracketing his mouth. His chestnut hair was liberally streaked with gray and he was underweight, although not as thin as he'd been the last time she'd seen him.

The sour twist to his features and the dead in his eyes were the biggest changes the passing years had wrought. He didn't look like he'd had a single moment of happiness in a long time.

Well good. He'd sucked the life out of everyone who'd loved him. He deserved his misery.

She approached, waiting to catch a whiff of the cheap whiskey he'd drowned himself in for the longest time. She wasn't sure if she should speak to him, not relishing the prospect of one of his drunken outbursts. On the other hand, better here than in the crowded lobby. Or worse, in front of Emma or her grandparents.

Miranda took a deep breath. "I don't know what you're doing here, but you need to leave." He stared at her impassively, and she stared back. "Okay, then. How about get the hell out before you upset your daughter. She deserves better tonight." She made no bones about sharing her contempt.

He continued to stare and she held her breath, steeling herself for his outburst. Instead, he treated her to a scathing glare as he turned on his heel and left the balcony. She followed him slowly, hoping like hell he had the good sense to walk out and not make another scene.

She made it to the lobby as the actors began lining up. Quickly scanning the crowd, she breathed a sigh of relief. He'd chosen to leave and managed to duck out before being seen.

From the way he looked at her, she knew he still held a grudge. He hadn't forgiven her for her alleged role in his wife's death.

"It's your fault," he'd spat at Renee's graveside. "You got her involved in that fucking theater in the first place. If she hadn't had to stay late for a damned rehearsal, she wouldn't've been driving home at midnight in the pouring rain. She wouldn't've tangled with a drunk driver and hit a tree. She wouldn't be dead if it weren't for you and that show. It's on you, Miranda Jenks. You and the Durango."

Well, there was a truth Ross would never know. And she understood him even as she loathed him.

On the drive home, she thought about how it was much easier it was for him to blame her and the Durango than to look in the mirror and admit he'd been a lousy excuse for a husband. Drunk more often than not, he'd neglected Renee and their daughter.

Miranda *was* responsible for getting Renee involved in the theater, hoping if she participated in the productions it would keep her too busy to continue drifting from one affair to another. It'd worked for a little while, and then Butch had gotten out of the Army and moved home. Having a young, good-looking neighbor had been irresistible to the lonely, love-starved woman. It didn't take long before Butch and Renee were doing the horizontal as often as they could.

Miranda turned onto the rutted drive leading up to the farmhouse on the Bar T Ranch, her small property that'd been in her family since before the Civil War. A three-story Victorian greeted her, and Miranda sighed at her ongoing, never-ending project. The constant repairs were irritating, but at the same time they were another way to fill the lonely hours when she wasn't at the Durango.

Replacing a rotting floorboard or repainting a dreary guest room beat the hell out of sitting by Tommy's grave longing for her dead son. Tonight she felt the need to talk to him before she went inside the silent, achingly lonely house. She needed to tell him about his all-grown-up friend's success. And maybe she needed to put voice to why she'd lied to the world about his friend's mother.

She turned onto the even bumpier drive leading to the family cemetery populated by Robards and Tumlisons, and Burneys and Jenkses stretching back almost two hundred years.

She parked outside the gate and sat a minute to allow her eyes to adjust to the light of the almost full moon shining down on the assortment of tombstones, some of which were in danger of falling over in the next few years if nothing was done to preserve them.

Miranda walked past the old monuments to a small grave in the back. The stone shone white in the moonlight its markings clearly visible in the silvery glow. "Thomas William Silva, Jr. August 7, 2001 - January 12, 2010."

Below the second line was a beautifully carved image of Tommy riding his beloved mare Rosie. Miranda sank down on the grass beside the headstone and crossed her legs in front of her. The only sound a warm June breeze ruffling the leaves of the nearby oak tree.

She sat quietly for a minute before telling Tommy about Emma's big debut. "Her dad was there hiding in the balcony. I couldn't tell if he was drunk." She paused. Did she really need to be telling this to a nine-year-old?

Miranda shook her head. She wasn't really talking to Tommy and she knew it. She'd always known it. She was talking to herself. Only sometimes, like tonight, it was easier to do it here.

"He's mad at me. I got his wife involved in the theater, and he blames me for her death. But he'd be hornets' nest mad if he knew I've been lying about where she really was that night. He'd blame me for covering up her cheating. Which is exactly what I've done. I've kept Renee and Butch's secret. I've protected their cheating asses. *Because Emma doesn't need to know."*

Miranda shifted on the hard ground. She wasn't concerned about Renee and Butch, though she supposed she owed Renee, who'd stood beside her during Tommy's long illness and death, and then singlehandedly pulled her out of a hellish combination of grief and addiction, setting her on the long road to recovery.

Miranda would be eternally grateful to her for that. But Renee wasn't alive anymore to care what the world thought of her, and Butch had cleared out within a matter of weeks of Renee's death, deciding the Alaskan oil fields were more to his liking than the fields two counties over.

Emma and her grandparents, Byron and Barbara Summerset, had been devastated by Renee's death and didn't need to have her faults aired for the world to see. Miranda loved those three people, especially Emma, with her whole heart. While she didn't much like herself for doing it, she would continue to lie to protect them from the truth.

She sure as hell wasn't protecting Ross. As far as she was concerned, he deserved to have Renee's adultery shoved in his face. The man was an idiot in so many ways. He'd fallen in the bottle for no good reason.

She'd know. She was an alcoholic, but a sober one, and staying that way was a 24/7 full-time job. Ross had been drinking heavily since Emma was in elementary school. The fool had thrown away his marriage and his child.

Miranda sat with Tommy for a few more minutes, soaking in the peace and solitude until her aching backside reminded her she wasn't twenty-two anymore.

She stood on stiff legs and leaned over and kissed the still warm headstone. "I miss you, baby. Bless you, wherever you are."

She stuck her hands in her pockets. Absentmindedly, she fingered the blue and white AA seven-year chip she carried with her everywhere. She'd been awarded that one last fall and was almost due for another.

Which reminded her. She had an AA meeting tomorrow afternoon at two.

She'd have to set the alarm much earlier to get the calves to the auction and back to the church basement on time.

She really *needed* to make the meeting tomorrow.

Chapter Two

Ross

Ross parked his car in the driveway in front of the beat-up old farmhouse he'd come home to last week. He looked down at his shaking hands, visible in the moonlight coming through the windshield. Hell, his whole body was trembling, screaming out for the alcohol he'd indulgently supplied it with for the better part of fifteen years. Going to the Durango tonight had been the acid test. It'd pushed his sobriety to the limit, but he was so hungry to see his daughter—even at a distance—after not seeing her for well over a year, he'd gone to the theater anyway. Now he was paying the price. It would be so easy to turn around and head for the twenty-four-hour gas station on the Interstate and pick up a six pack and a couple of bottles of cheap wine to tide him over until he could get to the liquor store for the good stuff. But that would undo nine solid months of hard work to get where he was tonight. Work he would have to repeat, starting over from scratch—if he even could. He'd barely made it the first time. He had no idea if he'd be able to give up his intoxicating lover the second time around.

He'd had to leave the alcohol behind if he was going to re-establish any kind of relationship with Emma.

Swearing out loud in the dark, he scooped his mail off the seat and stomped up the steps, dodged the rotten board halfway up the porch, and threw open the front door. He tossed his baseball cap on the hall tree and made his way to the kitchen where he dumped the mail on the table, turned on the light, and popped a pod of decaf in the coffee machine. It was a crap-ass substitute for booze, but coffee had become his lifeline since getting sober, and somewhere in

Colombia he was sure there was a mountainside full of coffee growers praying nightly for his sobriety to continue.

Though his hands were still shaking when he sat down with the coffee, the rest of him was beginning to calm down. But it would be hours before he could sleep. It didn't really matter, he thought as he sipped the black brew. He didn't have any burning reason to get up with the chickens. There weren't any around these days.

His chickens had gone the way of his cattle and hogs, sold at auction before he left the state nearly two years ago, the profits from the sale of his livestock used to bum around the country in his beat-up old truck. With no destination in mind, he'd drifted from place to place, picking up work here and there, but mostly he drank himself blind most nights as he tried to drown his sorrow. He'd lost his beloved Renee to a senseless car accident and his precious daughter to his own stupidity.

He sighed as he pulled the mail stack closer. It was mostly advertising fliers and credit-card come-ons. Nothing of importance. No, not quite. He pulled a bill out of the stack and used a steak knife to open it. *Ouch.* Even with halfway decent insurance, he'd run up one hell of a hospital bill.

A nearly fatal case of Covid would do that.

He tossed the bill to one side. He'd have to pay what he could, when he could, and hope his credit rating survived. He wished he could wave a magic wand and pay the whole thing, with bonuses for the selfless doctors and nurses who'd worked like dogs to save his worthless ass. They'd known damn well he was a drunk and he was immunocompromised by years of abusing his body, and they'd busted their butts anyway.

He'd been in Arizona when the pandemic first hit, so out of it the crisis barely registered. He hadn't cared enough to wear a mask or take the recommended precautions and found himself in a fight for his life when it spread like wildfire through the flophouse where he was staying.

He'd spent nearly a month in the hospital, struggling to breathe around the elephant sitting on his chest and thinking hard about the wake-up call Covid had been. "You've been given a second chance," his nurse admonished him the morning he was discharged from the hospital. "You need to do something better with it than rushing out to buy a bottle."

He'd agreed. As soon as he was declared infection free, he checked into one of the few treatment programs in Arizona his insurance would pay for. He'd gone from there to a working ranch in Montana that hired hard-luck cases like him.

Long days and physical labor were good for both his body and his troubled spirit. He'd spent nine months there, working as hard as his healing body would let him. He'd attended AA on almost a daily basis, and if not for the Red Rock and Emma, he would've been more than content to stay in Montana.

But it was time to be Ross Ellis again, to see what he could salvage of his life, his ranch, and his relationship with his only child. He would have to make amends to her somehow, and to all the other people he'd wronged during his many years of alcohol abuse.

He'd put off doing steps eight and nine while in Montana, since there was no way he could make amends to anyone there. He'd wronged a shitload of people in Texas, and he had to take those steps here. Now that he was home, he would address those steps on his road to recovery. He'd make that list and start making whatever amends he could.

He wasn't sure quite who to put on the list since he'd been an asshole to so many folks. Emma for certain. Some of his old friends around town. The pastor who'd reached out to him after Renee's death. It was too late to make amends to his father, or Renee.

The Summersets? He ground his teeth together. They probably belonged on the list. They'd taken his daughter in and given her a home when he was at his worst. They'd been critical and furious with him the past few years. Although he knew he should, he didn't want to make amends to them. He would have to talk to his sponsor about it. He glanced up at the clock. Too late to call him tonight. It didn't really matter. He'd see him tomorrow at the meeting and ask him then.

He finished his coffee and put his mug in the sink. He thought of the disdain on Miranda's face this evening at the theater and the way she'd ordered him "to get the hell out."

His lip curled as he pictured her standing there, her hazel eyes shooting sparks at him for daring invade her turf. The years hadn't been kind to her. Curly hair that was at one time a dark, rich brown was liberally streaked with gray, and a good twenty extra pounds padded what had once been a mouth-watering figure.

With a smile and a little makeup, her face might be pretty, but he hadn't seen her sport either in years. Not since her son died, come to think of it.

He tamped down the sympathy the better part of him wanted to feel for her. Hell, he was sorry about the kid. A shit thing to've happened, but Miranda had gotten Renee involved in the theater. It was Miranda's fault Renee was dead.

Miranda would not be on his making amends list.

No way in hell.

***

Miranda

"Come on, you no good son of a bitch. Get out of that trailer," Miranda snapped as she slapped the hardheaded calf on the rump. "Your buddy backed out like he was supposed to." The healthy-sized calf looked at her and mooed. The eight-month-old Beefmaster ought to bring good money this afternoon at auction, once she got him unloaded. "That's right. I'm selling your shitty ass and you can be somebody else's problem."

"What's the matter, Miranda? Your baby misbehaving for you?" Shorty, the old cowpoke working the auction chute, laughed and swatted the calf on the rump like she had.

The calf obediently backed out of the trailer and ran through the chute to the waiting pen. "How the hell did you do that?"

Shorty grinned wickedly. "I have the touch. You have any more you're bringing today?"

"Nah. It'll probably be a couple of months before I have anything else to sell."

Shorty's smile faded. "I don't know why you bother any more, as few cattle as you run these days."

Miranda tilted her head. "You know damn well why. So I can get the tax breaks for running a cattle ranch as opposed to living on country acreage. It's the only way I can afford to stay on my own land."

"Oh, I get that. I think it's sad, though, that you're not making more of a go of it. That ranch has been in your family forever."

"I'm doing fine," she assured him. "My day job pays the bills."

"So what about your neighbor? He ain't run any cattle on his place for over a year now. Didn't plant nothin' this spring, either. How's he gonna keep his place?"

Miranda's lips firmed. "Don't know and don't care."

Shorty winced. "Neither does anybody else in town, as far as I can tell. You gonna stay for the auction?"

"Not today. They can send me the check. See ya."

She hopped back in the truck and glanced at the dashboard clock. Damn. She would have to hurry or she'd be late. Larry, a retired rock drummer who'd been sober for almost twenty years, always began the meetings promptly at two, which didn't give her much time to get home, get cleaned up and back to the church hall on time. But she could make it if she tried.

She parked the truck beside the barn and left the trailer to deal with later. A quick shower and shampoo to get the dust out, a pair of black jeans and a black sweater in case she had to go backstage during the play, comfortable dark boots to stand in for hours, and she was good to go. She pulled her three-year-old Beetle into the church parking lot on the stroke of two and hustled into the fellowship hall, stopping to pour herself a cup of coffee and snag one of the donuts, which would have to suffice as lunch. She greeted a couple of regulars by name with a smile and sat down in the circle, juggling her coffee and the donut. Her eighth-grade history teacher waved and smiled sardonically at her from across the circle. "Lunching with us again, I see."

Miranda smiled. "I had to take a couple of calves to market this morning, Adam. and I have to work this evening. I'll take what I can get." She'd never get used to calling Mr. Lambert by his first name, but that was the rule in AA and she would abide by it, but it felt wrong.

"That's not healthy, dear," sweet Miss Loraine admonished her.

"Yes, ma'am." She'd known Loraine Bosch for years and secretly wondered if the dear old lady really had a drinking problem or was just looking for someone to talk to. But that wasn't something to ask, especially in a small-town group that wasn't especially anonymous. She could have had true anonymity if she'd wanted it. Any of them could. But it would mean driving all the way to San Antonio for a meeting. Besides, nobody ever talked outside this room. Ever. They respected one another's privacy. They respected one another, period. Each of them knew all too well what the others had faced and conquered. Not to mention what battles lay ahead.

And who they could call at three in the morning when the demons raised their ugly heads.

Miranda polished off the doughnut. "There's plenty if you want another," Larry said encouragingly.

"Thanks." She helped herself to a second and was sitting down when the door opened and an all too familiar figure strode in. She stared, shocked as hell as Ross scribbled his name on a name tag and poured a cup of coffee. So he'd given up the booze. Interesting. She wasn't sure she quite believed it, but she hadn't smelled it on him last night like she had so many times in the past. Nor had his reaction been that of a man under the influence. He'd been in control of himself. Cold, hostile, and pissed as all get-out, but in control.

Maybe he had gotten sober.

It would be interesting to see if he really had.

Or not. She looked again at his too-thin body. If he'd quit drinking, he should've regained more of the weight he'd lost over the years. He should look a lot better than he did.

He carried the coffee over to the circle and sat in the last chair. The extra chair, one more than the usual ten in the circle, meant that Larry must've been expecting him. The other attendees looked at him with varying expressions. Some of them appeared welcoming, others had more of a *wait and see look* on their faces. Some, like her, seemed to be having a hard time believing Ross really meant to stay sober.

Larry was his usual warm and gracious self. "It's time to get started. I'm Larry and I'm an alcoholic."

"Hi, Larry," they chorused in unison.

They went around the circle, dutifully introducing themselves and admitting to their addiction. Ross was the last one to speak. "I'm Ross. I'm an alcoholic. Boy, am I."

The group laughed quietly. Larry then read the twelve steps out loud and Melanie, a former stripper who'd recently earned her five-year chip, read from the Big Book. Then Larry opened the meeting up to discussion. "How was your week? How's everybody doing?"

Her old history teacher spoke up first. "I'm seriously considering backing out of the family reunion next month. My cousin emailed the schedule of events yesterday. Most of them involve drinking. That's the last thing I need to be exposed to."

"How do they involve drinking? Dinner at a restaurant that serves drinks? A get-together in a bar? A Hill Country wine tasting?" Miranda asked.

"All of the above and more. An afternoon wine tasting, a dinner-with-wine pairings, a pub crawl, lunch at a brewery, and so forth. I said something to my cousin about it and he said to come and not drink. As if."

"So don't go," Miranda said.

"Folks don't realize how tempting that can be," Melanie murmured.

"You've worked too hard to get sober," Larry added. The group nodded. "Anybody else?"

A few members spoke up. Miranda listened. Under other circumstances she might've mentioned how meeting up with her nemesis had thrown her off kilter, but with Ross sitting right there she'd be damned if she said anything. It would be interesting to see if he spoke this afternoon.

Larry looked around the group. "Anyone else?" he asked.

Ross raised his hand. "I'm new here and I guess I might as well go on and tell y'all what's going on. Let's be honest. Most of you already know me and know I've been drinking for the last fifteen years, and like a fish for the last ten of them. I finally got sober last fall after damn near dying of Covid."

Miranda sucked in a breath, as did most of the others in the circle. That would explain why he looked so unhealthy. The virus took an enormous chunk out of a lot of its victims, and if it had almost killed him, he was most likely still healing from that. "Are you all right now?" Miss Loraine asked.

"I'm a hell of a lot better than I was in October. It took me awhile."

"So what have you been doing with your time since then?" Bob asked.

"I worked on a cattle spread in Montana. Would've stayed, but for my ranch here and my daughter," he said candidly.

Too bad you didn't stay in Montana. Your daughter would be better off if you had.

"Anyway, I'm back and trying to move forward. I want to make a go of the ranch again. And I desperately want to reconcile with Emma."

The group nodded approvingly and several gave him a thumbs up. "So what's the first thing you're going to do to reach your stated goals?" Larry asked. "What steps are you going to take?"

"I've worked through some of the steps in Montana but not all. My next steps are numbers eight and nine." He took a deep breath. "I need to make amends. But I'm not sure who all to make amends to."

"Anyone you wronged or hurt because of your drinking," Larry said. "Unless making amends is only going to make it worse for them. It's not always an easy list to come up with."

Bet I'm not on that list. Miranda smiled inwardly.

"I've noticed," Ross said dryly. "The obvious one is my daughter. She had to live with a drunk for a lot of her life. I hurt her badly last year. So badly she slapped me in the face and said she hated me." He ran his hand down his face. "She probably still does."

You've got that right.

"She wouldn't be the first child or the last to hate an alcoholic parent. It's been five years and my daughter still isn't speaking to me," Melanie said ruefully.

"All right, your daughter's at the top of the list," Larry said. "Who else?"

Ross named off a few of his old friends and mentioned the pastor of Renee's church. "My in-laws, probably. I don't know about them. They were as shitty to me as I was to them."

Maybe he's right about them. Byron and Barbara had never hidden their antipathy toward him, especially after their daughter died.

"You don't have to complete the list in one sitting," Larry said. "Anyone else?"

Ross's face clouded. "The one I need to make amends to the worst is no longer here to make amends to."

Several in the circle nodded. Most of them knew what happened to Renee.

"It's hard. If she were still alive, I would find a way to make it up to her every day for the rest of her life. Even though I'm mad at her. Every time I think about how she died, I want to wring her neck."

"How so? How did she die?" Bruce asked. He was the newest member and one of the few who didn't know Ross's backstory.

"She was coming home late from a theater rehearsal in San Antonio. It was pouring rain and a drunk driver hit her. I blame her for that. If she hadn't stayed late at a damned rehearsal, she'd be alive today." He took a deep breath. "I blame her. I blame the theater, and I blame the ones who got her involved with it in the first place."

Ones? That was me, asshole. I got her involved in the theater.

Miranda shot Ross a *fuck you* look nobody else appeared to notice. At the same time, she was torn. He was laboring under a falsehood. An out and out lie she could correct with a couple of sentences. Did he need to know the truth? Did she need to tell him that his wife spent the last hours of her life in another man's arms?

No. If she told Ross the truth, it was bound to get back to Emma, and the Summersets. It would hurt them so badly, especially Emma. That took precedence over Ross and whatever telling him the truth would accomplish. But there was no reason she couldn't speak up on behalf of the Durango. "You say you're interested in making amends to Emma. Yet you bitterly resent the theater that's become one of the most important things in her life. How do you think you're ever going to make amends to her feeling like you do?" she asked.

"It's two different things," Ross snapped. "I can make amends to her no matter how I feel about the theater."

"Ya think?" Miranda asked quietly. "The minute she finds out how you really feel, you can kiss good-bye making amends or a reconciliation." She leaned forward. "That theater means everything to her. It was a lifeline at the lowest point in her life."

"It killed her mother," he said bitterly.

"It probably saved hers," Miranda said softly. "Here's a thought. Maybe if you knew more about the Durango and what she does there, you might lose some of the resentment and actually reconnect with your girl."

"You know, Miranda has a point," Miss Lorraine said, ignoring Ross's pissed off expression. "If it's something that means a lot to your daughter, it would be a good place to start."

"It certainly couldn't hurt," Bruce said thoughtfully.

Adam said, "What better way to reach out to her? To push past the resentment she's bound to know you feel, and become involved in something that means so much to her."

Ross shook his head. "I don't know if I can."

"Something else you don't have to commit to this afternoon. As long as you intend to reach out to her somehow," Larry said. "Any other thoughts?"

No one had anything else to suggest. They ended with the Serenity Prayer and most of the group hit the coffee maker for another cup. Miranda looked at her watch. It was a little early to head to the theater, but better early than late. She wished everyone a good afternoon and was almost to her car when Ross caught up to her, his eyes shooting sparks, and parked himself in front of her with his arms crossed. "What the hell was that all about in there? Telling me to get involved in that fucking theater? It's the last thing I want to do."

"All the more reason to do it," Miranda said firmly. "Or are you blowing out your ass about making amends to Emma?"

"No, I'm not blowing out my ass about making amends," he snapped. "But I'll be damned if I do it there. It's the theater's fault Renee's dead."

"Can it, Ross. That's ridiculous and you know it. It's not the theater's fault she's dead."

"Then who's fault is it? Yours? You're the one who got her involved in the fuckin' place to begin with."

"Actually, it was the *drunk* driver's fault. Which could've been," she pointed at the church, "any of us."

He scowled.

"All right, you wanna go there? You bet I got her involved with the Durango. She needed to get out of the house and away from her falling down drunk of a husband, and I helped her do it. Under the same circumstances I'd do it again in a heartbeat. You want to know what motivated her to say yes? Go look in the damned mirror."

Ross stumbled back a step. "She didn't need to get away from me."

"Like hell she didn't." *You and a string of lovers.* "You were drunk all the time and you know it."

Ross's stare could've melted ice. "Fine. I'm responsible. At least you think I am. I'm sure you're going to tell me what you think I should do about it."

She nodded. "You're sober. I'm guessing you're thinking straight these days. It's time you gave up your drunken delusions it's all the theater's fault, and admit it was a fucking accident in the rain caused by a *drunk driver* who took her.

"Quit using me and the Durango as your whipping boys. Quit trying to find something or someone to blame for a tragic car wreck. If you're serious about making amends to your daughter, do something for the theater she loves so much. I dare you to get involved at the Durango and use the theater to make amends to your daughter."

She moved to walk around him to get to her car, then stopped.

"Come to think of it, you need to make amends to the theater too. Thanks to your drunken outburst during a rehearsal full of teenagers, a couple of the kids quit the Academy and took their tuition with them." She walked past him and said over her shoulder, "I'm due at work." When she got to her car, she turned and said, "If you got the balls, talk to Josh Goldstein. Tell him Miranda sent you."

She got in her car and tore out of the parking lot, leaving him in a cloud of dust. She hoped she hadn't been overheard by anyone else at the meeting. She'd broken every rule when she threw Ross's drinking up to him. But it was past time for him to quit blaming her and the theater for the accident. If he kept it up, his daughter would never let him back into her life.

Now that Ross was sober and appeared to be determined to stay that way, she wanted him to have a relationship with Emma. The girl deserved to have a real father in her life. He was her only surviving parent.

To her surprise, she wanted it for Ross as well.

Chapter Three

Ross

Ross parked his truck in front of the dry cleaners halfway down the block from the Durango and stared at the old marquee gracing the front. His memory of the conversations he'd had with Renee were a bit spotty sometimes, but he distinctly remembered the afternoon she'd come home, excited the old sign had been installed in front of the "new" Durango, purchased by the rich husband of one of the actors. He hadn't cared one way or the other at the time, but now a wave of bitterness washed over him as he looked at the renovated marquee. *The damn place should have stayed dead.* His late wife would have been a hell of a lot better off if it had.

But the community theater had gained a second life and had become vitally important to his daughter, despite her mother's fate. Since he'd been dared to get involved in the theater, to find out what went on and why it was so important to Emma, he'd have to use it as a vehicle to make amends and find his way back into her life.

Damn Miranda. He'd never been able to resist a dare and she knew it.

Okay, time to show he meant to have his daughter back in life, and he'd do anything to make that happen. He locked the truck, straightened his shoulders, and marched up the sidewalk and into the theater. In the lobby he spotted Renee's younger brother Kevin at the concession stand fiddling with a case of sodas. Kevin's eyes narrowed and he looked at Ross bitterly. "Here to make another scene?" he asked snidely. "Here to embarrass Emma again?"

"If I wanted to do that I would have done it on opening night," Ross replied. He'd fully expected hostility from the Summerset clan.

"I left instead. The last thing I want to do is embarrass my daughter. Where's the guy in charge of this place?"

"What's it to you? The last time you were here he tossed you out on your ass."

Ross gritted his teeth. "Is he here this afternoon? Does he have an office in the back?"

"Damn it, Ross, I don't know what you want this afternoon and I don't care. Get the hell out before I call the cops."

"I can do that, of course. But I'm here at Miranda's behest. Does she need to get your permission? I think I have her number here somewhere." He got out his phone and started to scroll through his contacts.

Kevin's eyes widened and his face turned red. "*Miranda* told you to come? Well, hell." He pointed with his thumb. "His office is next door." He scowled, shook his head and went back to the sodas.

Ross went into the suite next door and down a hallway with small offices on one side and a large rehearsal room on the other. Most of the doors were open and there was a low hum he thought of as business sounds coming from the rooms. He peeked in the first door. A beautiful woman looked up, her smile fading as she stared at him. *Uh-oh.* She must have been here the day he'd thrown his drunken tantrum.

He vaguely recognized the woman in the second office, but remembered the man in the third office all too well. This was the guy who'd tossed him out on his ass. Ross gulped and took a deep breath before stepping into the office. "Mr. Goldstein? I'm Ross Ellis. If I could have a moment of your time?"

Josh folded his arms in front of him and looked him up and down. "What can I do for you this afternoon, Mr. Ellis?" He looked over Ross's shoulder. "You may as well come on in, Rachel. You're gonna want to know whatever he has to say."

The beautiful woman from two doors down stepped into the office. Josh gestured to a chair and Ross sat down. His palms were sweating and his heart was thudding against his chest. Which was ridiculous. He would present his case. If they took him up on his offer, fine. If they didn't, that was okay too. He took a breath. "I'm here this afternoon to see if I could volunteer at the Durango." He paused a minute, but neither Josh nor the woman said anything. "You know. Sell drinks or take tickets or whatever it is that you need doing." He hated feeling uncomfortable, and right now he felt like he was being examined like a bug under glass. He'd be damned if he said anything more.

Josh and Rachel looked at one another. "Why would you possibly want to volunteer here, Mr. Ellis? You don't have much use for the theater, as I recall," Josh said.

"More to the point, why would we want you?" Rachel added. "The last time you were here, you created the scene from hell and scared a roomful of kids. You accused the theater of costing your late wife her life and called your daughter a worthless bitch."

Ross's stomach roiled. "I called her what?" he asked.

Josh's brow rose and his eyes widened. "You don't remember?"

Ross ran his hand down his face. This was worse than he thought. "I was pretty far gone that morning."

Rachel murmured something under her breath that sounded like "you don't say."

"Listen, I'm sober now. Have been for over nine months. I'm not doing drunken scenes anymore. I'm going through the Twelve Step program, and two of those steps involve making amends for things I've done that were hurtful because of my drinking. The morning I was such a shit here at the theater is at the top of that list. I hurt Emma. Miranda said I cost you some students. Maybe I could make those amends by volunteering."

Josh started to shake his head. "I don't think so," he said slowly. "Sir, I'm sure you mean well," he said quickly when Ross started to speak. "But the last thing your daughter needs while she's up on stage is to have to perform knowing you're somewhere in the theater."

"You did a real number on her," Rachel said. "It was a good month before she would come back here. It took everything Jessica and Miranda had in them to persuade her to put herself out there and audition for *West Side Story.*"

"Okay, then." Disappointment warred with relief. He was off the hook. "I'll go." He would have to find some other way to make amends to his daughter.

"No, you won't," an all too familiar voice said from the door. "Sit your ass back down." Miranda stepped in and looked from Josh to Rachel. "You two are gonna listen to what I have to say before you send him out the door. He's here because I issued him a challenge. He needs to make his way back to his daughter and the Durango's going to be his way of doing that."

Wonderful. Miranda was going to do what she always did: put in her two cents. He wasn't off the hook after all.

She shut the door behind her and plopped down on the side of Josh's desk. "Normally I'd stay out of a conversation like this, but not today. Emma needs to find her way back to her father. She needs a reason to forgive him and let him back in her life. She seems okay on the outside, but she's not on the inside."

"Okay," Josh said slowly, and then tilted his head at Ross. "But what about him? What reason do we have to trust him around our patrons? I don't need to remind you he was a real prick that morning."

"I get that," Miranda said. "I remember the entire episode in vivid detail. Trust me when I tell you, I've known him since we were kids and I know damn well the kind of shit he's capable of. But I *know* he loves Emma, and he loved her mother. I also know up-close and personal what alcohol will do to a person—the kind of shit people do drunk, they'd never do sober, and how damned hard it is to get sober. Ross managed it. He's sober now, has been for a while. I'd like to think we're open-minded and accepting enough to give him a chance with his daughter."

Josh and Rachel sat silently, Josh's nose crinkling like he smelled something foul. "I think it's gonna bother Emma having him here while she's doing a show," Josh said.

"On the other hand, it might be good for her to know he cares enough to get involved here," Rachel said. She turned to Ross. "Are you really sober?" He fished his nine-month chip out of his pocket and handed it to her. "What's this?" she asked as she looked at it.

"It means he's been sober for nine months." Miranda fished a chip out of her pocket and handed it to Rachel. "Mine's for seven years. Going on eight."

Rachel looked at the chips. "Good for you. Both of you." She handed the chips back, and then sighed. "I don't know."

Miranda looked from Josh to Rachel. "Really? As badly as we need volunteers? You're willing to turn down perfectly good help? We need him, Emma needs him, and he and his daughter need our help. Everybody comes out ahead."

"She has a point." Rachel looked at Josh. "Okay, I'm in. I'm game if you are."

"I'll say yes, but with a couple of conditions," Josh stated. "One, Emma has to be comfortable with you being here, Mr. Ellis."

"She's not going to be, at least not at first," Miranda said. "She's gonna need some time to adjust."

"I can stay out of the auditorium during the performances," Ross offered. "I'll clean the bathrooms or something."

"Or you could work in the concession stand," Rachel said.

"Kevin's gonna love that," Ross murmured.

"I'll take care of Kevin," Josh said. "Fine. You do something in the lobby. The second is you always have to be on your best behavior. All the time. Polite and gracious to our patrons. *Do not* get into anything with any of the Summerset family. I'm going out on a limb letting you do this. Don't you dare make me regret it. They're gonna be pissed off enough about it as it is. I hate pissing off our patrons. I especially hate pissing off the generous ones." He leaned forward and looked Ross in the eye. "Can you do it?"

Ross nodded. "I can."

"Fine. We'll see you Friday night." Josh stood and offered his hand. "Good luck. You're gonna need it."

Ross shook hands with Josh and Rachel. Miranda fell into step with him as he walked to the door. "I guess I ought to thank you," he said. "They'd already turned me down."

Miranda's eyebrow shot up. "'Ought to'? Doesn't sound to me like you're thrilled."

"I'm not. I sort of agree with Josh. It's going to put Emma under pressure knowing I'm in the theater."

"So happens I agree with Rachel. I think it will mean something to her that you care enough about her to give your time to the theater knowing it means the world to her."

"I hope." He pushed open the front door and stepped out into the June dusk. "Still hot out here." He looked over and saw that she had a ridiculously big handbag with her. "Done for the day?"

"Heading home." They ambled down the sidewalk together.

"Long day?"

Miranda's shoulders twitched. "Probably longer than it needed to be. I spend a lot of time at the theater. More than I need to really. Beats being lonely at home."

"And jonesing for a drink?"

She was silent for a minute. "Yep," she said.

Ross looked at her curiously. "You've been sober how long now? Nearly eight years?" She nodded. "Does it ever get any better?"

"Eventually. But I have triggers that still make me want it so badly I can hardly stand it. If it gets really bad I pick up the phone and call Larry or my old sponsor from my San Antonio group."

"Whoopee. Something to look forward to."

"Sorry to tell you, but the monkey's never gonna be off your back entirely. I would've thought your AA sponsor in Montana would've explained it to you."

"He tried. I didn't quite believe him."

"Believe him."

He nodded, "Yeah, I'm convinced." He looked up and down the street. "Where's your car?"

"Around the block. I didn't want to walk through the back of the theater. They're using the rehearsal room with the exit door this evening."

Ross looked over the neighborhood. "Will you be all right walking alone? Is the neighborhood safe?"

"It's fine. Thanks for asking."

They stopped alongside his truck. "This is my bucket of rust." He looked over at Miranda and thought about the lonely evening she faced. He faced one as well. "Want to go out for a little supper?" he asked before he could stop himself. She stopped and stared at him, a question in her eyes. "My treat. I owe you for getting me in the door. They wouldn't have budged otherwise."

Her eyes danced and she bit her lip. "Thought you weren't all that happy they said 'yes'."

"I'm not sure it'll work, but I'd be a fool not to try. Anyway. How about it? Dinner someplace you like."

"Someplace I like." She seemed to be thinking about it. "Or should we go someplace I don't like?"

He rolled his eyes. "You know what I mean."

"Okay, then. There's a really super Chinese place right on the highway just south of Pecan Valley."

"Ming Flowers? Never been there, but I know where it is. Tell you what. I'll run you around back and then follow you there."

She nodded. He unlocked the doors and she hopped in his truck. "Sorry about that," he said when she sat on a split in the cushion.

"Don't apologize. At least it's clean."

She pointed to a side street. He made the corner and came upon a large parking lot taking up most of the block. "All for the theater?"

"Yes. The auditorium holds nearly three hundred, plus the actors, musicians and crew. That's a lot of cars on performance night."

He pulled into the lot. "You still in the Volkswagen?"

"Which one? I've had four of them." She gestured to a sporty green Beetle about halfway down. "The latest rendition."

"Cute."

"I'll try to keep you in my rear-view mirror, but if we get separated take the Pecan Valley exit stay on the access road. It's right there."

"I'll find it."

He watched her hop out of the truck and walk toward her car, her hips swaying with each step she took.

She'd worn her hair loose today, with wild, gray-streaked curls spilling across her shoulders and down her back. Tight jeans hugged her too-lush curves and legs that seemed to go on forever. The shapeless sweater did nothing to flatter her generous tits or the luscious cleavage he suspected lurked within.

Her face was pale in the gathering dusk, faint lines around her mouth and fanning from her eyes giving away her age. But her features were delicate and even, and he knew from living with Renee a little makeup would go a long way toward accenting Miranda's face in a pretty way. It wouldn't take much, he thought as he started his engine. A little makeup, a flattering blouse, and mousy Miranda could be something else.

Chapter Four

Miranda

Miranda stepped into Ming Flowers and inhaled appreciatively. The aroma of garlic and Chinese spices tickled her nose as Ross stepped in behind her and shut the door. The sun had sunk low in the sky while they sat in an aggravating snarl close to the Alamodome. Sitting in the congestion had given Miranda plenty of time for second thoughts about dinner with Ross. She was supposed to be angry with him. He'd done a lot of things that were really shitty. He seemed to have changed, but she wasn't sure she could trust those changes were real. She reminded herself it was only dinner. They weren't on a date. She wasn't making a lifetime commitment.

Still, she felt a little tingle where his hand rested lightly on her waist.

The hostess escorted them through the half-occupied restaurant past empty steam tables to a booth in the back. With an apologetic smile she handed them menus. "Except for the Mongolian Barbecue, we haven't gone back to serving buffet-style yet." Then she handed them an order form and a pencil. "Write down what you'd like and we'll make you a plate. It's unlimited and the same price as the buffet."

They took the order forms and the pencils. Miranda went down the list and jotted down her favorites. Ross stared at the menu for a moment. "What's good here?"

"The moo goo gai pan is to die for. You can also count on the egg foo yung. But remember, you can order a lot of different things and they'll adjust the portion size and bring them all to you. It would be a good night to experiment. Don't forget the Mongolian

Barbecue. As soon as I have a few things written down, I'm having them cook a bowl."

She went down the menu and listed six of her favorite items, and she jotted down the items she wanted in the stir fry. The server picked up their lists and went to the kitchen, handing the lists to the cook working the stir-fry. From where they were sitting, they could watch as the cook assembled their stir-fry dishes from the items listed and tossed them out on the huge iron griddle, sprinkling them with their choice of sauce as the vegetables sizzled. "Smells good," Ross commented. "Good thing we came somewhere you like."

"Wiseass," she murmured.

Their server brought them the stir-fry first and then returned with plates heaping with the items listed. They were silent for a few minutes as they dug into their food. Miranda had missed lunch and hadn't realized how hungry she was until now. She glanced across the table to see Ross eating like a man who'd been starved for a month. If her memory served, Renee had complained more than once about his lack of talent in the kitchen. His inability to cook might be part of why he was so thin these days. His ranch was even further out of town than hers. It wasn't like he could run around the corner and pick up a hamburger.

They cleaned their plates and Ross signaled their server, who good-naturedly gave him another order form and pencil. "Didn't like it a bit, did you?" she teased as he wrote out a second list.

"It's the first decent meal I've had all week," he admitted. "One of these days I'm going to teach myself to cook. In the meantime, I owe Mr. Stouffers and Mr. Banquet a debt of gratitude."

"Ugh." She didn't try to hide her disgust. "Nasty."

"It's either that or starve." A shadow crossed his face. "Emma cooked for me a lot before she left. I didn't appreciate her until she moved out."

"Sadly, that's usually the case." The server came by the table and Ross handed over his second list. "So, what are your plans for the farm?" she asked. "Are you going to rebuild a herd or farm the whole acreage?" She figured Ross needed a break from thinking about Emma and his failures as a father. Maybe talking about the farm would provide it.

He looked at her and his expression said he knew exactly what she was trying to do. Apparently he was willing to go along with it.

"I'm not sure yet. I'm working with a consultant from the State Extension Service to formulate a plan for the farm."

"How much is that costing you?"

"Not a penny. Your tax dollars at work." He winked.

"How 'bout that? So what all are you doing with the consultant?"

"Consulting." Ross looked at her deadpan.

"Fun-ny. Seriously, what are they helping you with?"

"All kinds of things. He came out yesterday and took some soil samples. Gonna see what shape the fields and pastures are in first. He said with the rain and sitting fallow for a while, the fields might not be in the bad shape I thought they were."

"On the other hand, you and your dad before you, overgrazed and overplanted for years. Does the consultant know?"

"He took one look at my fields and figured it out. But he thinks the time off and the rain last summer and fall might have gone a long way toward restoring productivity. The pastures can probably be revived with fertilizing and then seeding coastal Bermuda over the Bermuda that's already there. I can give the grass a few months to grow before I start rebuilding a herd."

"Sounds like a plan. What kind of cattle do you want to get this time? Back to Herefords?" The herd he'd sold off was heavy on Herefords with a few Simmentals.

"I'm thinking about switching to Beefmaster, like you've raised the last few years. Have you had good luck with them?"

"The handful I still raise, yes. Shorty was fussing at me the other day for running so few. He thinks I need to make more of a go of the ranch."

He shrugged. "No real reason. You haven't had much interested in it since you and Tom split up and you have a day job to pay the bills. Unlike some of us, who have to make a go of it or forget about eating." He smiled crookedly.

"Or you could grow your own food." She returned his smile with one of her own. "Speaking of, what shape are those fields in? The ones you farm? What will it take to salvage them?"

"Not sure yet. Depends on the soil analysis. Peanuts would help restore the soil. Strawberries and watermelons would bring in money too. I'm in no hurry. I can't plant until next spring anyway."

Miranda raised her eyebrow. "What are you living on, then?"

"I have a little money left from selling my herd, and a little I saved in Montana, but I'm plowing through it fast. I'm looking at getting a day job."

"A lot of farmers and ranchers have them." She thought of how to ask, and decided to dive right in. "Tacky question. Are you qualified to do anything other than farm or ranch?"

He made a face. "Nothing I really enjoy. But I was pretty good behind the counter at the feed store in Devine once upon a time. Sold a lot of stuff folks didn't know they needed until I got hold of them. I'll probably hawk ranching supplies for a while."

"You could do a lot worse."

"I sure could."

The server brought his second plate of food and he dug in. Miranda sat quietly and watched him eat. She'd always liked watching a man enjoy his meal, and tonight was no exception. Ross was enjoying the second plate of food as much as he had the first. This close, the ravages of years of drinking combined with the lingering aftereffects of Covid were even more apparent. The too-thin body, his pinched features, the pallor underneath the superficial tan, the aging his face had undergone in the last few years—he looked like a man who'd been through the wringer. But tonight, he'd lost the sour expression he'd worn at the theater, and the deadness in his eyes had been replaced with a twinkle. His smile reminded her of the boy she'd gone to high school with. The one she'd crushed on in secret, hoping nobody noticed. The one who'd been so appealing to her when she was seventeen. The one who was still appealing to her now, despite all the heartbreak and drama she'd witnessed over the years.

Her contempt for him was fading, although it hadn't disappeared entirely. He was the last man she should feel attracted to, especially knowing he was early in his sobriety. If things went south at the Durango and with Emma, that could be trigger enough to send him back into the bottle.

Ross forked up the last of his stir-fried shrimp and bacon. "That was wonderful. The food at the Richardson Ranch was abundant and filling, but it wasn't really all that good."

"Is that the ranch where you worked when you got out of rehab?"

"Yeah. The counselor at the Arizona rehab facility put me on to them. Billy Richardson's father was a recovering alcoholic and started hiring folks trying to stay clean, and believe me, there are always plenty of alcoholics and addicts for them to pick from. On-site AA meetings and you damn well better have left your habit behind when you come through the front gate."

"How do they know?"

"Billy's a remarkable judge of character and can sniff out bullshit from a mile away. The men and women he hires are the real deal. Some stay for years, and several of the married couples they employ met and married there." He looked down at his empty plate. "If it hadn't been for my own ranch and Emma, I would have stayed on gladly."

"I'm glad you came back." *Whoa. Where had that come from?*

Ross looked at her ruefully. "If you mean it, you're the only one."

She reached across the table and put her hand on his arm. "That'll change. It may take some time, but sooner or later Emma's going to give you another chance."

"I hope so. But I don't know. Didn't the lady in the AA meeting say her daughter hadn't forgiven her yet?"

Miranda's lips twitched. "Her drinking had nothing to do with it. That's what happens when you seduce and then marry your son-in-law. Not that sonny boy wasn't seriously willing to go along with his wife's sexy mama."

Ross winced. "How long did that last?"

"They're still married."

"You know, I can see where it might be a bit of a problem."

They looked at one another and burst out laughing. But as they looked into one another's eyes, their laughter faded. Miranda was suddenly gripped with an intense attraction to Ross. Her breathing hitched and her heart thudded in her chest. From the look in his eyes, the interest wasn't one-sided. His gaze was locked to hers as he breathed deeply and then blew it out, never breaking eye contact. Miranda tried to look away but couldn't, and he did he seem to be able to either.

What in the hell was going on?

Their waitress broke the spell, bustling to the table with a couple of fortune cookies and the check. Ross whisked the check from the tray and handed her one of the cookies. Miranda broke open her cookie. "'The greatest achievement in life is to stand up again after falling.' I think I knew that."

"I think you did, too. Let's see what I got." He broke open his cookie and read the fortune. "'The change you started already has far-reaching effects. Be ready.'" He stared down at the tiny slip of paper. "Damned if that's so." He laid the paper on the table.

Miranda grabbed the paper and read the fortune again. "From your lips to god's ears." She kissed the paper and flung it into the air. "I happen to think it's right. You've made some mighty big changes in your life in the last few months. Those changes are going to make a difference far into your future."

"I sure hope so."

"You're not convinced."

"Not even a little."

"I guess only time will tell." She glanced down at her watch. "Speaking of, it's getting late and we have an hour's drive ahead of us. Thank you so much for dinner and the company. I thoroughly enjoyed both."

"Thank you for persuading Josh and Rachel to change their minds and let me volunteer. I hope to hell this plan of yours works."

"So do I. Your daughter needs you. Badly. Even though she tries to make out like she doesn't."

"She'll have me from now on, if she wants me."

"Give her time to get to know the new Ross. She'll want her dad sooner or later."

The waitress brought back Ross's card. They stood and walked in silence to their cars. Ross's hand was warm and firm on her waist. This close, she was achingly aware of the tall, man walking beside her, his shoulders broad and his body powerful despite the ravages it'd suffered. Miranda felt herself starting to come alive from his nearness. She fought back the sudden urge to turn and wrap her arms around him and feel his closeness. *This is Ross Ellis,* she reminded herself. *Renee's husband. Emma's father. The man who wreaked so much havoc in Renee's life. The man who devastated Emma in a drunken tantrum.*

The man who's kicked the habit. The man who would do anything to make amends to the daughter he loves.

She was really attracted to this new version of Ross Ellis.

The cars were parked in a dark corner of the parking lot. She unlocked the door and turned to Ross. "Thank you again for a delightful dinner."

He stared at her for a minute before framing her face between his hands. "I'm gonna regret this, but I can't help myself," he said softly as he lowered his lips to hers.

Heaven, sweet heaven, she thought as they met in a kiss that was equal parts gentle and passionate. Hesitant at first, they nipped and nibbled as they each other. Ross began gently, holding her like she was a delicate flower, his arms tender around her waist and hers tentative around his neck. But their tenderness quickly turned to passion as their bodies responded to the closeness. Miranda tightened her arms around his neck and opened her lips, inserting her tongue to dance with his. They moved closer until their bodies became plastered together. Her nipples tightened beneath her thin knit shirt and she began to dampen between her legs. She could feel his cock swell against her stomach and his muscles tighten. She slid her arms down and around his body, reveling in the masculine hardness of his chest against her swollen nipples and his muscular back beneath her fingers. His hands explored her waist before drifting lower, cradling her butt and pulling her even closer. His hands were large and his fingers strong on her eagerly responding body. Her heart pounded, and her breathing sawed raggedly. She never wanted this to end. Not if she could help it.

They held onto one another for long moments, tasting, touching, and savoring. It'd been a long time since she'd been in a man's arms, and probably as long since Ross had held a woman in his. When Ross raised his head and stared down at her, his eyes were glazed and his breathing was ragged. She watched as the desire slowly faded from his face and consternation took its place. "Do I apologize?" he asked quietly.

"Hell, no. Best kiss I've had in a long time."

"Okay, then. I won't feel bad about it."

But he did. She could tell it troubled him. "You have nothing to feel bad about."

He smiled ruefully. "It's not that I feel bad. A little disloyal, maybe, but not bad."

She didn't know what to say to that. So she stood up on her tiptoes and kissed his cheek. "Your first night at the theater's this Friday, right?"

He swallowed. "This Friday. If Kevin doesn't sic the Summersets on Josh and make him change his mind."

Miranda laughed softly. "You don't know our Josh. He doesn't scare easy, and Rachel's even fiercer. You'll be fine. Do you want a Durango t-shirt to wear?"

"I'll get one later. See you Friday."

Miranda nodded and got in the car. Her fingers were trembling on the steering wheel and her heart was still pounding against her ribcage. It'd been all she could do not to throw herself back into Ross's arms for another spectacular kiss. She hadn't been this moved by a kiss in a long damn time. And, if she was being honest with herself, never. Not even Tom Silva's kisses had affected her this way. For Ross to say kissing her made him feel guilty... What a kick in the fucking ass.

Miranda gunned her engine as she pulled onto the expressway. Talk about feeling like a worm. Not about kissing Ross, that had been wonderful, but about her continued dishonestly concerning Renee. She couldn't really fault Ross for feeling disloyal. She'd bet her next paycheck he hadn't been with anyone since Renee died. Between the heavy drinking, the Covid, and the stay on a ranch in the middle of nowhere, his opportunities had been limited. For that matter, it'd probably been years since he even kissed another woman. Whatever his faults, cheating on his wife was not among them. It was natural he'd feel a little disloyal to Renee.

Too bad his late wife didn't deserve his loyalty.

Chapter Five

Ross

Ross swore as he crossed over the loop and immediately hit a slowdown on the highway leading into the city. San Antonio traffic sucked, no two ways about it. He shook his head and slammed on his brakes, shooting the finger at a snot-nosed kid in an old Kia poking along well below the speed limit. The appointment with the Extension consultant had run long and he'd gotten a late start. Miranda told him to park in the back lot but to get there in plenty of time so that he didn't run into Emma backstage before the show. "She's not happy right now with the thought of you volunteering. You don't want to upset her with a face-to-face before she has to perform."

The Kia driver shot the finger back at him as she pulled out of his way. He got in the fast lane, which really wasn't all that fast, and made his way into San Antonio and toward the inevitably congested downtown. He couldn't imagine having to fight this every day of the week the way Miranda did. He got that the theater meant more to her than just a job. But to drive in this shit every day? If it were him, he'd volunteer every so often to feed his soul and find some other way to make a living.

But that was Miranda for you. She threw herself into everything she did. She'd given everything she had to her marriage, and when her relationship with Tom went south she put the same passion into raising Tommy and doing everything possible for him after he fell ill. She'd lost her way for a while after his death and the divorce, but once she'd sobered up, the Durango became the new focus for her considerable time and energy. The theater had taken the place of her family, and probably in some ways had become her family. It had been good for her, even if it hadn't been good for Renee. The appealing, engaging, passionate woman he'd kissed the life out of the other night was the Miranda he remembered from back when, before grief and alcohol had gotten hold of her.

And boy, he'd kissed the life out of her.

Ross ran his hand down the side of his face. That kissing business wasn't going to happen again. Not that it hadn't been damn good. Her body had been warm and lush against his and her lips had tasted of sweet fortune cookie and sexy, willing woman. It had been great at the time. It hadn't been so great hours later, tossing and turning at half-mast while weighed down with a shit pile of guilt. He was Renee's husband, for god's sake. He had no business finding pleasure in another woman's arms. Especially Miranda's. He wasn't sure what in the hell that was about. Renee's best friend and a recovering drunk to boot. Even minus the guilt, she was the last woman he needed to get tangled up with.

He inched his way through downtown, took the exit to the Deco District, and finally pulled into the parking lot behind the Durango. He stared for a moment at the back door and watched as Rachel and a woman who looked a whole lot like her got out of a bright blue Dodge Challenger and then disappeared into the theater.

Okay, this was it. No more ruminating about the kiss that shouldn't have happened. He had to get his head out of his ass about this place and go in there and prove something. He had to show his daughter he'd changed and could be the father she deserved if she let him. He had to show his in-laws he was a new man. Despite the antipathy between him and Renee's parents, for way too long they had been there for Emma when he hadn't, and they'd had Emma's ear for years. If he couldn't get them on board, it was doubtful he would get past "go" with his daughter.

He had to prove something to Miranda and the theater crowd, and he had to show them their faith in him wasn't misplaced. He sure had something to prove to himself. Tonight was going to be a challenge of epic proportions, even worse than coming here the first night of the production. If he could get through this and not commune with Johnny Walker or Jim Beam afterward, he could stay sober through anything.

He hoped to hell he didn't blow it.

He went in the back door and wound his way through a mostly empty rabbit warren of dressing rooms and prop shelves until he found himself on the steps leading down to the auditorium floor. Despite the freeway traffic, he'd arrived early enough not to run into Emma backstage and upset her before the performance. His footsteps echoed in the mostly empty auditorium as he walked up the side aisle. The house lights were on, and either the light or sound technician was already at the board. He nodded a greeting as he passed by and the girl nodded in return before returning to work.

He stood in the door taking in the eerily quiet auditorium. It felt alien, even more so than it had when he'd snuck into the balcony last week. He felt alien as well. He looked down at the nondescript shirt and jeans Miranda suggested he wear instead of his usual western style shirt and tooled belt and boots. "The last thing you want to do is draw attention to yourself or stand out in any way," she'd explained. "You want to fade into the background." *And not get noticed by the Summersets.* She couldn't have said it any louder if she'd shouted it into his ear.

He made a pitstop in the restroom right off the auditorium, and damn it, his hands were shaking. This was ridiculous. He could do this, honestly he could. He wandered into the lobby and found Miranda and Kevin Summerset whispering animatedly about something. Him, probably. Kevin looked up and glared.

Probably wouldn't be the last one he'd get tonight.

Miranda looked over and nodded. She was dressed in black jeans and a black sweater, the same as she'd had on last Saturday, and a comfortable-looking pair of ankle boots. Her wild mane of curls was tied back and she wore a head mic and carried a clipboard with her phone clamped to it and a pencil tied onto the hole in the clamp. She was dressed for work and comfort. While her jeans outlined her hips and ass to perfection, unfortunately, the sweater did nothing to show off her breasts.

Still, she was rockin' it tonight. She always had.

Too bad she was so completely off-limits.

He crossed the lobby, ignoring Kevin's distain, and greeted her with a smile. He gestured to the clipboard. "No app for that?" he teased.

"Nope. Low tech for me." She glanced down at the phone. "Seventy-five minutes to curtain," she murmured into the headset.

He barely heard a feminine voice say something that sounded like "Roger."

He looked from Miranda to Kevin. "I'm here to help. What would you like me to do?"

"Go home," Kevin murmured under his breath.

Wonderful. Kevin was going to be an asshole while he'd been lectured to behave.

It was going to be a long evening.

Miranda looked at Kevin with squinted eyes. "You can start by helping Kevin set up the concession stand. Rachel said something about taking tickets or something when the audience starts to show up. Don't worry. We'll keep you busy." She looked at Kevin. "Remember what I said. We don't need a scene here tonight." She disappeared into the back.

Kevin looked at him with thinly disguised hostility. "You can start by unloading these sodas into the refrigerator."

He nodded and made quick work of the sodas while Kevin unloaded candy bars and popped the first popper full of popcorn. Kevin gestured to a case of beer. "Can you handle those?" he asked roughly.

"Yeah," Ross said. It would be later when he had to smell the stuff that would be the challenge.

He loaded the beer into a large tub of ice. By then a few patrons had begun to drift in and Rachel and Josh had both made an appearance in the lobby. Neither greeted him with much enthusiasm and he wondered if they were having second thoughts. Rachel came up to the counter and eyed him. "You know how to make change?" she asked.

"I'm good at it. Once upon a time I worked the counter at a feed store."

"Good. The girl who normally works the souvenir booth got an evening job and won't be back. You can sell t-shirts and pins. At least for tonight."

And get the hell off Kevin's radar.

"Are you sure you want him working a money box?" Kevin asked.

Ross rolled his eyes. "I'm a drunk and a crapass father, but I never stole anything in my life. I paid for every bottle I ever swilled.

You can trust me with your money," he said calmly. He had the pleasure of watching Kevin's ears turn red.

She nodded once. "Good to know. Come with me."

He followed her to a counter off the entrance to the auditorium. The shelves behind the counter were stacked with Durango Street Theatre and *West Side Story* tees, theater pins and Christmas tree ornaments were displayed in the case. Rachel slid a money box into a drawer built into the case. "Common sense. Don't leave the drawer open and don't leave the counter unattended. Someone will spell you for a restroom break once the show starts. Price list is taped on the counter. Any questions?"

"Do I stand here and take the money or do I actually sell the product? You know, talk up the merchandise and nail down sales."

Rachel looked flummoxed by the question. "I never thought about it. If you think you can sell it, knock yourself out."

She left him to it and a couple of minutes later his first customer wandered up. He ended up selling them two more shirts than they originally wanted, as well as an ornament. Business was sporadic, but by the time the prelude started his customers had made a considerably dent in both stacks of shirts. He'd kept an eye peeled, but hadn't seen Byron, Barbara, or anyone resembling Kevin's new wife. Just as well. They were bound to be as hostile as Kevin, and unlike their son, they hadn't been instructed to be nice.

Rachel came five minutes after curtain and locked the money drawer. "You can assist Kevin if he needs help restocking. I'll need you back here during intermission." Her eyes flickered to the diminished stacks of shirts. "I guess we need to order some more."

She didn't seem all that wowed by his selling expertise.

After he went to the restroom, he found Kevin busy replenishing the drinks and popcorn. Kevin gestured to another case of beer. Ross pulled the case open and unloaded the beer into the tub. Together they replenished the sodas in the refrigerator. "How much for a bottled water?" he asked tersely.

"A dollar."

Ross put a dollar on the counter and helped himself to a water. Kevin loaded the popper and started it going. He leaned against the counter and crossed his arms in front of him. "It's not going to work, you know. Volunteering here."

Ross raised an eyebrow. “It’s not going to work with her or with you?”

“With any of us. You’re being here watching Emma’s only upsetting her.”

Ross pointed to the auditorium. “If it’s not my imagination, that’s her singing. Am I watching her? Am I in any way interfering with her performance?”

“Just having you here’s upsetting her. It’s no way to make amends for your assholery.”

Ross raised his chin. “Then how would you suggest I do it?”

“Stay out of her life from now on.”

“Not gonna happen,” Ross said calmly, hoping his desire to punch in Kevin’s face didn’t show. “Look, Summerset, I get better than anyone what kind of an ass I’ve been to her. I was there. I remember. I was a shit in ways you don’t even know about. But I have it on damn good authority my daughter misses me and needs me, even though she may think she doesn’t. As wonderful as her grandparents and you and your new wife might be, y’all aren’t and never will be her father. She’s already lost one parent. She doesn’t need to lose her other one. Maybe this will work and maybe it won’t. But I’ll be damned if I bow out simply because it would be nice and convenient for the rest of you. Got it?”

Kevin’s jaw muscles jumped. “Whatever.” He turned his back and ripped open another case of sodas.

Ross’s hands were trembling as he started bagging popcorn. Every doubt he’d had about this rose up and slapped him in the face. Emma didn’t want him here. His hope of a reconciliation with his daughter was most likely doomed. His chest burned and the old craving grabbed him by the throat. *Just a little bit. Just a nip is all it would take.*

Sweat popped out on his brow. *No. That’s the last thing you need to do.* He swiped his hand across his sweating face and looked up to find Miranda looking at him with outright worry on her face. She took one look at him and grabbed his arm. “Come with me,” she whispered as she shot Kevin a withering look. “Damn it, I told you to *behave,*” she hissed at the younger man.

Ross stumbled out from behind the counter. From the corner of his eye, he saw Kevin’s eyes widen and his hands go up in a conciliatory manner. Miranda pulled Ross across the lobby and out the front door. The sultry air hit him in the face and he took a deep breath. "I'm okay. Honest. I need to go home. This isn't gonna work."

"No, you're not okay. Far from it. And you're not going anywhere. You're within an inch of driving away from here and finding a bottle." He looked at her and opened his mouth to deny it. "I remember what it feels like and I know every sign. Now what did he say to set you off?"

"The truth. That I'm upsetting Emma by being here." He looked at her helplessly. "I told him I wouldn't leave, but maybe it would be better if I did. The last thing I want to do is mess up her performance."

"You're not messing up anything. It's Kevin you're upsetting. Not Emma. She didn't act like she cared all that much one way or another."

Ross felt himself smile crookedly. "I'll stay. I don't mind upsetting that sanctimonious little prick."

"Attaboy." She scanned his face then asked, "Are you gonna be all right?"

"I'm not going to leave here and cuddle up with Jim or Johnny. Not that it wouldn't feel mighty good about now."

"*No,* Ross. You've come too far. Damn, it's still hot out here. Let's go inside. I gotta get back to work."

He followed her back into the theater. Miranda marched over to Kevin, and from the look on her face the guy was about to get an ass-chewing. Ross took his place behind the souvenir counter and a moment later Josh came by with the key to the money drawer. "Everything all right?"

"All good." He pointed to the shirts behind him. "Can you get some more tomorrow?"

"I'll see what I can do."

The house lights came on and patrons flocked to the lobby, lining up in front of the concession counter and both bathrooms. He managed to move several more shirts and a couple of the pins. The house lights had dimmed and the popcorn and soda-laden audience was drifting back in the auditorium when he glanced over and spotted his in-laws in what looked like a heated conversation with Josh. *Uh-oh.* They must have been in the audience. From the skewering glares they were sending his way, they weren't pleased to see him here.

Seemed no one could tell them to "behave" as he and Kevin had been.

His jaw clenched so tight it hurt. The Summersets had written some mighty big checks to the theater and no way was Josh going to risk losing those. If they told Josh to send him out the door, then Josh would most likely listen. Ross wasn't sure how he felt about that. For years he'd resented the Summersets and their far-reaching influence. But if they provided him an excuse to leave a situation that was becoming increasingly uncomfortable, he'd be damned if he argued about it.

Miranda came out of the auditorium, took one look and walked over to the Summersets. Well, hell. She was going to bat for him again. It would be interesting to see how the Summersets reacted. They'd known her for many years. She and Renee had been friends a long time, and unlike him, they didn't appear to hold her responsible for getting Renee involved in the theater or her subsequent death. If Miranda prevailed and he got to stay, he was going to owe her that much more.

Which wasn't the most comfortable feeling in the world.

The house lights dimmed for the second time and the music started. Miranda kept talking. The Summersets looked across the lobby at him skepticism written all over their faces. Finally, Byron shrugged. With one more scathing look in his direction, they returned to the auditorium.

Miranda to the rescue yet again.

He shut the money box in the drawer and straightened the considerably smaller stacks of shirts. Rachel came by a couple of minutes later and locked the drawer. "Do you have anything you need me to do until the show ends?" he asked her.

He spent a few minutes straightening the bathrooms and helped Kevin put away the uneaten candy bars. Rachel showed him to a small cubby off the lobby that had once been an office and he spent the rest of the second act reading the latest Ken Patterson thriller on his phone. Josh stuck his head in the door. "The curtain's about to come down. Time to sell a few more shirts."

Ross took his place behind the counter. The auditorium was filled with applause as the actors came out to take their bows. Then the entire cast came pouring out of the auditorium and lined up across the lobby to shake hands with the audience.

Renee had loved the accolades, even though she never got any further than playing in the ensemble. "It's so nice when they appreciate all the hard work we put into it," she'd gushed. "It's the most exciting thing ever."

Maybe if he'd appreciated her a little more, she wouldn't have needed accolades from strangers at the theater.

Ross swore to himself. Surreptitiously, he scanned the actors as they took their places in line, looking for his daughter, and was rewarded a moment later when she came through the auditorium doors, looking grown up and startlingly different in the black wig. She was smiling up at a handsome cast mate, who was flirtatiously smiling right back at her. Ross ground his teeth together. It was all he could do not to march over to them and demand an introduction to the upstart.

But he couldn't do that. He'd given up the right to be a part of his daughter's life and would have to earn it back...if he could.

He could tell the minute she spotted him. Her smile melted like ice cream on a hot sidewalk and she hightailed it to the other end of the line of actors. What little hope he'd had left he would make any progress tonight beat a hasty retreat.

Emma wasn't budging.

He dragged his gaze from his daughter's retreating back and turned his attention to a young father who wanted a tee for his daughter. By the time the actors had finished shaking hands and escaped backstage, the stacks of shirts were almost gone. Ross felt himself deflate as the desire for a drink roared back.

Tonight had been a fucking dismal failure. Surely, Emma would see and hear about the Summerset family's undisguised hostility. He never expected any help from them in his quest for a reconciliation with his daughter. Now he knew he could anticipate outright opposition and maybe even sabotage.

Johnny and Jim were looking better by the minute.

Josh came by a few minutes later and retrieved the money box. "Come with me and count this if you would. I want to get out of here."

"Hot date?"

"Nah. I have a husband and a couple of kids waiting for me at home."

"Gotcha."

They went by the concession stand where Josh picked up the second money box. They went to his office next door. Ross made quick work of counting the cash from the lobby kiosk and totaling the checks and the credit card receipts. He filled out a deposit slip and put it all in the money bag for the bank. "To the penny," he said as he pushed the envelope across the desk.

Josh was finishing up as well. "Not to the penny, but close enough." He looked at Ross. "Thanks for your help this evening."

"You're welcome. I hope the Summersets weren't too hard to deal with."

"Miranda's the one you need to thank. She told them that Renee was the last person who'd want to see you and your daughter at odds and that they owed it to their dead daughter to let you give it a shot." Josh looked at him curiously. "Has Miranda always been your champion?"

Ross huffed out a laugh. "Ah, hell, no. I've been on her shit list for years 'cause a the drinking. I'm surprised she'd take up for me with the Summersets. And with you and Rachel, for that matter. I guess she has to. This was her idea, and then our AA group gave it a thumb's up."

"You're in the same AA group? I thought it was supposed to be anonymous."

"In Pleasanton? Not really."

"Oh. Huh, I guess not. Well, thanks for the help. Will you be back tomorrow?"

"Tomorrow, and Sunday, and for every performance until Emma gets that I'm not going anywhere."

Josh nodded, Ross waved and left the office suite. The theater was still open, but if he went through the back he might run into Emma and he was afraid another rejection would push him over the edge. Instead, he took the long way, walking around the block. He longed for some peace and quiet and hoped he had the strength to drive past the grocery stores, and quick stops where he could get his hands on some alcohol.

Miranda was leaning against his truck with a rueful smile on her face. "Tonight sucked." Her tone was matter-of-fact.

"Ya think?" he asked a little bitterly.

She shrugged. "We knew it was going to. The important thing is you stuck. You showed the Summerset clan you mean it. You're coming back to this theater tomorrow and doing it again and again until the Summersets get the message, and your daughter's speaking to you again." She pointed her finger at him. "You aren't gonna drink. You're not touching the shit. Right?"

Ross shut his eyes. "From your lips to god's ears. I'm gonna try. I hope Larry doesn't mind a late phone call." He looked at her feeling helpless. "I'm close, Miranda. Too damn close. It scares me."

Miranda looked at him with understanding. "You are close, aren't you? I'm sure Larry wouldn't mind a phone call. But that's not gonna be necessary. You're gonna be with me tonight. Not like that," she added dryly when his mouth dropped open. "We're gonna be together as friends. We're stopping at that little diner off the expressway south of downtown and we're eating the supper we both missed. I'm throwing in a milkshake for me and you probably would enjoy one too. Then we're going back to your place, where we're gonna talk or read or watch Netflix. I'll bunk in your comfortable guest room and go home in the morning. Tomorrow afternoon we'll go to AA before we come back here. Sound like a plan?"

He nodded numbly. "Why are you doing this? You don't have any use for me."

"And you don't have much for me," she countered. "I'm doing it because you got off the sauce and your daughter needs you." She hesitated. "Besides, I owe Renee. If it hadn't been for her, I'd either still be wrapped in a drunken haze or dead. Helping you and Emma is the least I can do to repay her."

So the hot kiss had nothing to do with it.

Or maybe she just wasn't going to own up to it. "Well, for whatever reason, thank you."

"You're welcome and I'm hungry. Take the Hot Wells exit and stay on the access road."

He nodded and got in the pickup. She drove by a minute later and he fell in behind her.

Chapter Six

Miranda

Miranda put on her blinker and took the exit leading to the small mom-and-pop diner she'd been to a few times in the past. She glanced in her rearview mirror not quite sure Ross would follow her. He was close tonight. Too close for comfort. This evening had been rough, and she was beginning to wonder if she and the others at AA had made a mistake in suggesting he volunteer at the Durango. It was bound to push a lot of buttons. He resented the theater already, and he'd had to face Kevin's outright hostility as well as the Summersets' objections. And then his daughter had stayed as far away from him as she could. The way Ross was feeling, it could go either way.

She hoped to god he chose sobriety.

He followed her off the expressway and she breathed a sigh of relief. He was going to let her help him tonight. She was going to be his friend and help him resist alcohol's call. His friend. That was all. She wasn't going to kiss him again. She wasn't going to hold his hard, warm body in her arms or run her fingers down his muscled back. Getting involved with her was the last thing he needed. He was in the fight of his life right now. If he continued at the theater, that fight was going to get even harder. He didn't need the distraction of a romance, or even meaningless sex. It was the last thing she needed. To get involved with her best friend's widower, a man she'd lied to through her teeth to for years.

Even if the thought of sex with him was as tempting as hell.

They parked side by side and Miranda took Ross by his trembling hand and led him into the little restaurant. The tantalizing aroma of fried food and apple pie tickled her nose as they waited by the door. A few of the booths were filled and a scurrying server motioned for them to sit anywhere. Ross pointed to a booth in front of the window and they slid in across from one another. "This okay?" he asked.

She looked out the window at the cars racing down the expressway. "I love looking at all the lights. I never realized how dark the ranch is until I went to work at the Durango and was in the city so often after dark. It's especially awesome from a few stories up. Josh's husband used to live in a fourth-story condo south of downtown and he had us all over for a party once. The view from his place was spectacular."

Ross made a face. "Never my cup of tea."

"What was never your cup of tea? The lights?"

"The city. Too big, too crowded, too everything. I think Renee missed it."

"She never acted like she did. She never said one way or the other."

The server brought water and a couple of menus. He flipped his open and scanned the contents. "What's good this time of day?"

"Their breakfasts are always good, but I've been craving one of their burgers for the last three days."

"That good?"

"That good."

They gave their order to the server. Miranda hid a smile when he ordered extra cheese and a topping of jalapenos. Renee had always said he had a cast iron stomach, and her friend knew what she was talking about. Miranda ordered a topping of refried beans and *pico de gallo*.

Their server disappeared. Ross settled back and clasped his hands together in front of him. "They aren't shaking as bad," he observed.

She laid her hand over his. "Only a little. Give it a few more minutes. If that doesn't work, the burger will."

He nodded. They sat silently for a long moment. "I still resent the theater," he said quietly. "I still blame her involvement with the theater for her death. But now I have to wonder if it was the theater she loved so damn much, or if it was the city itself that was so alluring."

Oh, hell. It was neither. Again, she questioned her decision to keep the truth to herself. And again, she decided not to be honest with him. "I doubt it was any particular love of the city," she said slowly, hoping a half-truth would satisfy him. "She married you knowing she'd be living on a farm for the rest of her life. She always said she liked the quiet and being able to see the stars at night."

"So it was the theater itself," he said slowly. "She wanted to be there and not at home with me and her daughter." His expression was bitter as he looked across the table. "She'd rather be kicking up her heels in a damned show."

"Why do you suppose she felt that way?" Miranda stared across the table, meeting his eyes unflinchingly. She wasn't going to sugarcoat this part of the truth. Ross stared back his lips tight. "Say it. Tell me why she didn't want to be at home with you in the evenings." He kept staring across the table. "You're never going to come to terms with her death until you admit to the truth about your home life."

"It wasn't that bad," he snapped.

"The hell it wasn't. For crying out loud, quit denying it. Admit the truth. She was living with a drunk. Some days an out and out falling down drunk. Ross, you need to own up to it. She wanted to get away from you and she had damn good reason."

He was quiet a minute. "Was it that bad?" His voice was low and rough. "Was being home with me really that awful?"

Miranda continued to hold his gaze. "She thought so." She sighed. "I know what you're thinking. You were always a nice guy. At least when you were sober. But a lot of the time you weren't sober."

"But I never raised my voice. I never threw things or hit her. Even when I was drinking."

"True, you were a nice drunk, as drunks go. At least until after she died. But you were a drunk. She said on the days you drank, you'd be half gone by four, and totally blotto by six or seven. She never knew if you were gonna be passed out by suppertime. She couldn't count on things being okay at home. But she could count on the theater. That was her escape."

At least sometimes it was.

She wasn't going to think about Renee's other avenue of escape.

Ross was silent for a minute. "I don't know what you want me to say."

"I don't want you to say anything. I do want you to do some thinking about it. Now, enough of that depressing topic," she said briskly. "Let's find something else to talk about. Sitting here rehashing ugliness isn't accomplishing a damned thing. Not when you're having a shitty day to begin with and feeling booze calling your name."

"Not talking about it won't make it go away."

"No, but beating it to death won't either."

"Fine. So, how 'bout them Cowboys?" he asked dryly.

"I wouldn't know. I don't follow pro football." They both laughed a little.

But she did follow pro basketball, and they were in a semi-serious discussion of the current season of the Spurs when their server brought out their big, juicy burgers. Miranda watched with satisfaction as Ross dove into his, practically inhaling it. Good. A stomach full of food would go a long way toward alleviating his desire to drink. Their conversational detour didn't seem to have set him back too much, but she would do her best to keep the rest of the evening light. He'd had enough stress for one day.

She polished off her burger, but gave him half of her fries. They indulged in huge milkshakes and she snatched the check before Ross could get to it. "My invitation, my treat. You can pick up the next one," she said as he started to object.

"You think there'll be a next one?" He raised his eyebrow.

She nodded. She sure hoped so. As unwise as spending time with him would be, she knew he needed a friend. She remembered how much Renee's steady friendship helped her get back on her feet. The problem with being friends with Ross was, if they continued to spend time together, sooner or later they were bound to act on the attraction they felt.

She paid the bill and together they walked to their cars. "I'll meet you at your place," she said.

"You don't have to do that. I think I'll be okay."

"You think. But you don't know. Until you're sure, it wouldn't hurt for you to have somebody there with you. As wonderful a sponsor as Larry is, he'd probably rather be home with his pretty wife. See you on your front porch." She hopped in her car before he had a chance to argue.

***

Traffic was light once they got out of town, and it took them less time than usual to make the drive. A light rain was falling by the time they reached the Red Rock Ranch. She waited patiently on the wide front porch until Ross joined her. He pushed the door open and motioned for her to enter. The house had been cleaned recently, but was still shrouded in an atmosphere of absence and neglect. "It's not a home any longer," he said quietly as she looked around the living room. "It hasn't been a home since Renee and Emma left." He turned to her with tears in his eyes. "They made it a home. With them gone, it's only a roof over my head."

"I felt that way for a long time too. With Tommy dead and Tom gone, it was a big old house. Nothing more. Still is, in some ways. I hate to say this, but you'll get used to it."

"It will be a home again when Emma comes back. If Emma comes back."

"Even if you and she reconcile, I doubt she'd ever come back here to live." She sat on the sofa. "Ahh. It feels good to get off my feet. As I was saying, the university's on the far north side of San Antonio. It's over an hour's drive one way. It's a long drive to the theater, and a lot of days she's at both. It's more convenient for her to stay with her grandparents."

"Real damn convenient," he murmured under his breath.

Miranda turned around and gave him the honesty. "Yes, it was convenient while you were drinking, and then when you disappeared. You owe the Summersets a lot and you know it," she added gently.

"Boy, you're not gonna let me get away with any shit tonight, are ya?" He grinned at her crookedly. "Some friend."

"Nope. No shit goes unchallenged. I can be your friend and still be honest." She looked around the room. "What do you have around here to kill a few hours? I'm not sleepy and you don't seem to be."

"The usual. Cards, dominoes, a few old board games. Some of Emma's video games. Movies. Netflix." He stepped closer. "Or I could kiss you again. See if we feel the same way we did the other night. See if we want to take it a bit further."

She ignored the temptation to take him up on it and took a step back. "Ross, I don't think so."

"Why not? I'm lonely. You're lonely. What could it hurt?"

"It could hurt plenty. You're trying to face down the temptation from hell right now. The last thing you need is sex with a fellow drunk muddying the waters. Besides, it's Renee you're lonely for. Your wife. Not your neighbor from one farm down. The last thing I need is to be her stand-in tonight. My ego in that area's fragile enough as it is."

He looked disappointed but not surprised. "Not even one little kiss?"

"Not even one little kiss."

"Okay. I guess it's Netflix." He sat down on the sofa and gestured for her to take the adjoining chair. "Get where you can see the television. And Miranda."

"Yes?"

"You were wrong about one thing. You might've been a stand-in for Renee, but you sure as hell would've been a wanted one. Just sayin'."

She shot him a smile. "Thanks. I guess."

It was silly how much the small compliment pleased her.

They surfed through the latest offerings and settled on a brand-new series neither of them knew anything about. He became quickly engrossed in the story, but her attention wandered despite the clever plot and dialogue. She didn't know what the hell to do. If he continued to believe the Durango was responsible for his wife's death, he would continue to resent it, and Emma would feel it. It would stand in the way of their reconciliation. But as lovingly as Ross clung to Renee's memory, she was afraid that telling him the truth about his wife's infidelity would drive him straight back into the arms of the lover he cheated on Renee with: Johnny Walker. She honestly didn't have a clue what was the right thing to do.

Whatever she did, the situation had "disaster" written all over it.

***

Miranda stood in her usual place in the back of the auditorium and watched with a critical eye as the curtain came down on the Sunday afternoon performance of *West Side Story.* She grimaced as she glanced down at the long list of notes she'd made during the performance. Things had been decidedly "off" this afternoon. The curtain had been late going up, cues had been missed, a mic wasn't turned on in time, a couple of the dance routines had suffered missteps. Minor slips the audience probably didn't catch, but she saw them, and they bothered her.

She was glad Jessica hadn't been here this afternoon to see the errors in her carefully choreographed dances. Even intermission hadn't gone well. Kevin had run short of beer, much to the displeasure of a few of their younger audience members, and Ross had completely sold out of shirts, which was going to disappoint several of the children whose parents had waited until after the show to make their purchases. Whoever was ordering the shirts had yet to catch on to Ross's skill behind the counter. Supply was not keeping up with demand. She would mention it in the staff meeting Tuesday and hope she wasn't tasked with doing the ordering.

She glanced out at the kiosk in the lobby where Ross stood ready to sell pins and Christmas tree ornaments, and fend off the complaints of disappointed customers. He would do it well, with a measure of tact and diplomacy she hadn't known he was capable of. Nor had she appreciated his tenacity. After a pep talk from her and encouragement from the AA group, he'd gritted his teeth and gone back to the theater for the Saturday evening performance, and to the Sunday matinee as well. He'd steered clear of Kevin, ignoring his scathing glares, and sold the hell out of the merchandise. He'd stayed miles away from Emma, but the girl could hardly miss his presence. One week later, he'd come back and done it all again.

He was making his point. He was back and he wasn't going away any time soon.

Miranda had to admit, he didn't seem to be making much headway. Kevin continued to grace him with withering glares, and Emma ignored him. It seemed like he was beginning to earn Josh and Rachel's begrudging respect for the money he was earning them, but they continued to regard him suspiciously, not trusting him to come in sober. But it had only been two weekends. The production had six weeks to go. A lot could change in six weeks.

At least Miranda sure hoped it would.

The cast took their bows. She spoke into her headset, and asked for a brief meeting with the cast and crew once the audience cleared out. The actors filed up the side aisle. Miranda caught Emma's eye and winked. She was relieved when Emma smiled and winked back. Either the girl hadn't realized Miranda was behind her father's involvement at the theater, or she didn't care. Miranda didn't know, but she'd bet her July paycheck it was the former.

Emma wasn't going to be amused when she found out.

The crew carried out their post-production duties while the cast greeted the audience. Then everyone took a seat down front and Miranda spent twenty minutes detailing the afternoon's errors and how they needed to be corrected on Friday. "I don't think these were overtly obvious to the audience," she said in conclusion. "But if they're not corrected during the next performance, they will be. Remember, our audience has paid us the highest of honors. They've parted with some of their hard-earned money to see a quality performance. That's what they deserve and that's what we'll deliver. So have a good week, and we'll see everyone Friday night for the best performance ever."

The crew scattered and the cast made a beeline for the dressing rooms. Miranda put fresh batteries in her headset and put it away in her desk drawer. She locked her cubby and was on her way through the back to the parking lot when Emma fell into place beside her. The girl had removed the dark wig and washed off her stage makeup, and was back to her usual youthful self. She smiled over at Miranda. "So we really blew it this afternoon?" she teased.

"Hardly. I've seen really blowing it and today doesn't qualify. But it wasn't as tight as it should have been. It's like everybody was a little hungover or something."

Emma made a face. "Or a lot hungover. I wasn't there, but a bunch of them went to Thirties last night and closed the place down. Drunk on their asses, according to Amy. They had to call a string of Ubers to get 'em all home."

"Ah, the good old days. There are times I still miss drinking, but I sure don't miss the hangovers." Miranda had never made her drinking or her recovery a secret around Emma.

"Something I've yet to experience. And may not ever. I'm scared to death to drink. You know, with my family history. It seems to run in the Ellis gene pool," she said.

"It runs in your family? It's not just Ross?"

"Nah. Mom said Granddaddy drank a lot, but was good at hiding it."

"Why didn't I know this?"

"Not something we're real proud of. Wait, no, I didn't mean—" She blushed and stammered to a halt.

"It's okay, honey. Nobody's proud of being an alcoholic."

"Still, I'm sorry."

They stepped out of the theater. The late afternoon sun beat down and heat shimmered off the sidewalk. "You want to grab an early supper somewhere?" Emma asked.

"What about your grandmother? Won't she have your dinner ready?"

"Babs and Pops are up at the lake for a few days. Babs frets about me, but I told her if I get tired of cooking I'll mooch off Letti and Kevin." Her face darkened. "She forgets how much cooking I had to do after Mom died."

"So let's do it. Go somewhere where we're not cooking or mooching. Got any ideas?"

Emma put her finger to her chin. "Would you rather do new and trendy with itty-bitty servings, or a home cooking kind of place with enough leftovers for tomorrow?"

"Plan B, Plan B," Miranda laughed.

"Then let's go to that old diner on Broadway close to the loop. The one that lists the vegetables on a chalkboard in the entry."

"Works for me."

They got there as a line was starting to form out the door. But Emma told the hostess they were willing to take a tiny table in the middle of the crowded dining room, and their wait was brief. Miranda scanned the menu, which hadn't changed in years and quickly decided on the seafood platter. Emma went for a heaping pile of fried chicken. "I'd get the meat loaf, but Babs makes a better one. She's going to teach me some evening when I'm not at the theater and don't have my nose in a book."

"When will that be? Ten years down the road?"

"There are days it feels like that."

"I think I know the meat loaf. Your mother used to make it."

"She did."

"She called it her comfort meat loaf. She brought a lot of it to me after Tommy died."

"I don't remember that."

"No reason why you would. You were only nine or ten and thinking about other things." Miranda took a deep breath as a memory intruded. "She also brought it to me the first night I got out of rehab. She made me eat and then put me in the car and took me to my first AA meeting. Sat right beside me for the whole thing." She paused. "I owe your mom a lot. She's the one who got me into rehab and then into AA. I'd have never gone otherwise."

"Don't know why she couldn't have done the same for Daddy," the girl said.

"She tried. The catch is, I wanted to sober up. Way down deep, I didn't want to keep drinking. Until last year, your father didn't want to quit. All the rehab and all the AA in the world is as useless as tits on a boar hog until somebody wants to quit."

"So you really think he wants to quit now?"

"I do."

"Forgive me if I seriously doubt it. He had years to quit and didn't." Emma looked at her impatiently. "What makes you think he really wants to quit now? How do you know he's not sobering up long enough to come to the theater and then going home and tying one on?"

"Because he's sitting through every AA meeting we have in Pleasanton. He's coming to the theater and putting up with your indifference and Kevin's hostility, and going home afterward instead of to a bar. He has a nine-month chip in his pocket that's about to become a ten-month chip. I'm not his sponsor, but sometimes I've helped him when the temptation's especially bad. You can't fake sober at eleven at night."

Emma looked at her, astonished. "You're helping him? I thought you couldn't stand him."

"I've not been a fan, nor has he been one of mine. But my objection to him was mostly his drinking. If he's willing to go through the hell of quitting and staying sober, then I have to do what I can to help him."

"Why? Why do you feel you have to help him?"

"Because that's what one drunk does for another. And because I owe your mother. She loved him and I think she'd want me to help him now."

She did love him. Never mind she cheated on him right and left.

"You're a better person than I am. Not only do I not intend to forgive him, I don't appreciate his coming around the theater. I don't know what he's trying to accomplish."

"How much do you know about AA and twelve-step?"

"Not much. Something about going through twelve steps to try to stay sober."

"That's the gist of it. Two of those steps involve identifying the people you hurt by your drinking and then, if at all possible, making amends for what you did. Not only apologizing with words, but actually doing something concrete and physical to make amends. Obviously, your father's drinking hurt you in ways even he can't imagine. He hurt the theater as well. The stunt he pulled cost them several Academy students. I dared him to get his ass to the theater and do something concrete for you and the Durango. He didn't like the idea much but the AA group thought it would be a good thing. So he's—"

"Wait. What? *You* put him up to volunteering at the theater? Damn, Miranda, how could you? I thought you were on my side."

"I am. Which is exactly why I did it. You need your father back in your life."

She could see Emma grit her teeth. "I don't need a rat-bastard drunk back in my life." She glared across the table at Miranda. "You were there that morning. You saw what he said to me in front of everyone. You saw him call me a bitch like my mother. He can call me what he wants. But he called my mother a bitch and I'll never forgive him for it."

"He wasn't the only one doing some name-calling that morning," Miranda said gently. "Was he?"

Emma looked at her defiantly. "Well, he is a worthless prick." Her eyes filled with tears. "I miss her, Miranda. I miss her every damned day of the world."

"I know you do." Miranda held her gaze. "So do I. But the bottom line is she's gone now and she's never coming back. So let me ask you this. Do you want to be down your other parent too? Yes, Ross was a drunk and did some despicable things while he was under the influence. But he's sober now. He's not a worthless prick any longer. He would like to be the loving father you had as a child, before the booze got hold of him. He's trying like hell to show you he loves you and needs you. And, honey, you need him, whether you know it or not."

"So tell me this. That day he was such an asshat in front of my dance class, he was going on about how it was all the theater's fault Mom died. Does he still feel that way? Does he still resent the Durango and my involvement there?"

"At this point, yes." Emma opened her mouth and Miranda held up her hand. "I've already told him he's not going to get anywhere with you as long as he feels that way. Which is the other reason I...we thought it would be a good idea for him to volunteer. Maybe if he gets an idea of what goes on there, he might get over the resentment."

Emma looked at her lap. "I'm not sure it would make any difference if he did. I don't think I have it in me to forgive him." She glanced up at Miranda. "He doesn't deserve it. He might've been a loving father when I was a kid, but I can barely remember those days. He did too much over the years. I mean, Mom was so wonderful, she was everything she was supposed to be and did everything she was supposed to do. And then for him to do the things he did. Neglect her all the time. Neglect me all the time."

Oh, Emma. She wasn't that wonderful. Not really.

The thought of voicing that, of telling this trusting child the truth about her mother sent a shudder through Miranda. The last thing Emma needed was to lose faith in Renee the way she had Ross.

So again, Miranda chose to go with dishonesty. "You still need to forgive him," she said gently.

Emma's eyes flashed. "He doesn't deserve it."

"Did I deserve it? I know you're too young to remember, but I was as bad a drunk as your father. Your mother didn't judge, she helped. I've learned an important lesson over the years you might want to think about. Sometimes we don't forgive someone because it would be better for them, we forgive them because it would be better for us."

Emma tilted her head. "Why?"

"Because hate, resentment, and rancor eat us up from the inside. Like it did me. I don't know if you remember Tommy's father."

"Not really."

"Well, he rabbited the minute we found out Tommy had cancer. Up and left us. Said having a sick kid was more than he could handle. I hated him with everything in my being. I hated him all the time Tommy was sick and after he died when I was falling into the bottle. Part of my recovery involved forgiving him. It didn't matter anymore to him, he was long gone, but it was instrumental in my recovery to forgive him and let it go. You might want to do the same with your father. It doesn't matter if he deserves your forgiveness. You're not doing it for him. You're doing it for you."

"Whatever."

Their server brought their heaping platters and they dug in. Miranda choked back a crushing wave of disappointment. She'd gotten nowhere. Her words had fallen on deaf ears. Emma was nowhere near ready to forgive Ross. She didn't know if the girl would ever be.

Ross would have to hang in there and hope for the best while she would have to keep on lying about Renee.

Chapter Seven

Ross

Ross handed over the small t-shirt and smiled down at the young girl. She was beaming, but telltale streaks on her cheeks gave away her emotional response to the production's heartbreaking ending. "Did you enjoy the show?" he asked quietly as he counted out change to the girl's father.

"Oh, yes," the little girl chirped. Ten or eleven, she was fresh-faced and sweet-looking, much like Emma had been at that age. "I loved it!"

Ross ignored the painful cramp around his heart and smiled at the girl. "The sad ending didn't get to you?"

She looked at him impatiently. "It's *supposed* to get to you. Like *Gone with the Wind* and *Les Miserables.* They were wonderful."

Her father shrugged his shoulders. "She loved *Cabaret*, too. Damned if I get it."

Ross's lips twitched. "I guess *Brokeback Mountain* and *Evita* are next."

"Probably." The father and daughter wandered off.

A young couple having a date night bought a pair of shirts, and an older couple bought a shirt and an ornament. Ross looked with satisfaction at the shrinking but still substantial pile of shirts on the shelf behind him.

It'd taken a couple of weeks, but someone finally snapped to and doubled the t-shirt and ornament order. Unless there was a real run on them, the supply should last through the weekend. He didn't know, and wasn't about to ask, but he hoped the merchandise sales were at least partially making up for the tuition they'd lost due to his tantrum.

Selling t-shirts was about the only thing he was accomplishing at the Durango.

He made a few more sales. The audience drifted out a few at a time and the actors disappeared one by one into the back. He'd been so busy he hadn't noticed when Emma left, and whether she'd been in the company of the young actor who seemed quite taken with her, although she didn't seem all that interested in him. Tonight it was Rachel who collected the money boxes. "You want me to help count? I've been helping Josh," he said to her.

"Sure." He followed Rachel to her office. As usual, the merchandise box reconciled to the penny and the concession stand was a little off. Rachel looked at him curiously. "Josh mentioned that you get it perfect every time. How do you do it?"

"Dunno. I guess I learned how when I worked part time years ago for a feed store in Devine. Started there again a couple of weeks ago."

She looked up in surprise. "I thought you were a farmer."

"I am. But I sold the herd last year and let everything go and need an income until I can get it going again." He smiled ruefully. "I'm gonna be busy."

"Too busy to come here?" she asked.

"No. I'm not dropping this." Even if he was getting nowhere he could see.

"Okay." Her face and her voice were expressionless, and he had no idea if she was pleased he was staying.

They finished with the money, and she locked it in the safe. Josh stuck his head in the door. "I'm outta here." He grinned wolfishly. "Both kids managed to get invited to sleepovers tonight. Cameron and I actually have the house all to ourselves."

Rachel winked. "Have an orgasm or two for me, will ya?"

Ross choked. Did she really say that?

"Have a couple for me, too." Amy came up beside Josh and made a production of looking him up and down. "Jesus, what a waste."

"Cameron doesn't think so." Rachel smiled wickedly.

Josh grinned and his ears turned red. "On that note I'm gone. See you Tuesday."

He ducked out. Rachel and Amy looked at one another and laughed. “We embarrassed him,” Amy sputtered. “I guess our filters are on the blink.”

“He’ll live,” Rachel said. She turned to Ross. “Sorry if we were a little raucous for you.”

“Nah, I’m fine.” Actually, he was a little envious. The theater people were tight. They teased, they partied together, and they enjoyed one another’s company. Everyone involved with the production was part of that camaraderie. Theater personnel, actors, crew. Even the ensemble and volunteers were included. Everyone was part of the Durango family.

No wonder Renee had loved it so much. No wonder it was so important to Emma. It gave them a sense of belonging. They were valued and included. They were part of something bigger than them, important and fun.

Something they sure as hell hadn’t gotten on the farm from him.

Ross pushed the uncomfortable thought to one side and listened with half an ear as Rachel and Amy made plans to meet up with some of the cast at the bar down the street. His first thought was to wonder if Emma would be joining them. But he’d heard Thirties ran a tight ship when it came to minors, and his daughter was underage. He wondered if he would be welcome in the Durango circle. Probably not. He was there on sufferance, not because he’d endeared himself to anyone at the theater.

Besides, he was a drunk with only ten months of sobriety under his belt. The last thing he needed was to go to a temptation-laden bar.

Maybe Miranda would want to go out for a late meal. They hadn’t been back out since the night he’d been so close to falling off the wagon. They’d watched Netflix until four in the morning and slept late, her in the guest room. She’d gone home, and he hadn’t seen her since, except for AA and the theater.

He had to admit she’d been right to turn him down. The last thing either of them needed was to land in bed together, even though the thought had been mighty tempting. Miranda’s warm, sexy body curled up next to his, their lips entwined, his cock buried deep in her shapely lushness. Yes, it had been most tempting.

Still was.

He went down to her cubby and poked his head in her door. She was fumbling with the batteries in her headset. Her face was pale and unsmiling, and deep circles rode under her eyes. Her expression was distant and troubled. She looked like she was a million miles away.

He couldn't claim to know her all that well, but he was sure something was wrong. He watched her fumble for a minute. "How often do you have to change those?"

She looked up, startled. "I didn't know you were there." She looked down at the headset. "After every show. The actors change theirs as well. Can't risk a failure during a performance." She slid the second battery in and pulled the covering over it.

"You want to go somewhere for a bite?" he asked.

She looked up and shook her head. "I'm gonna pass. It's been a long week and I wouldn't be good company."

"If you say so. At least let me walk you to your car."

She nodded, put away the headset, and locked up her office. They walked through the halls in the back of the theater passing nearly empty dressing rooms but for a couple of the ladies in the ensemble who were gathering up their things.

Miranda led him through the rehearsal room to the backdoor that led into the parking lot. Together they walked across the mostly empty lot to her car. "Thanks," she said as she clicked open the door.

"You sure I can't tempt you with a late meal?" he asked softly. She shook her head. "Will I see you tomorrow at AA?"

"I'll be there. See you tomorrow."

She slid into the car and headed out of the parking lot. Deep in thought, he wandered toward his truck. Something had been off tonight. She hadn't smiled, she hadn't asked him how he was doing, and she hadn't doled out her usual words of encouragement. In fact, he hadn't seen her at all this evening except in her office. Which wasn't the norm. Far from it. She made it a point to speak to pretty much everyone on performance night whether she needed to interact with them or not.

But not tonight. She'd not been herself, far from it, and it made him wonder what was going on.

He was worried about her.

Maybe she'd bring it up in AA. If she didn't, he'd talk to her afterward, either at the church or at the theater. Something was wrong tonight. If it was still wrong tomorrow, he would see if he could help her with whatever it was. He'd do it gladly.

She'd done so much for him.

He owed it to her to return the favor.

***

Ross pulled into the church parking lot next to Miranda's Beetle. He was a few minutes early but she was even earlier. He walked across the lot and into the fellowship hall. Miranda was already seated and was juggling a donut and a cup of coffee. He slapped on a name tag and snagged coffee and a donut of his own and sat beside her. She looked up and nodded her head solemnly before turning her attention back to the sticky donut. No smile, no sarcastic crack, no asking after his week.

Okay. Whatever had been bothering her last night was still on her mind.

Now the question was whether she would bring it up in the meeting or if he would have to talk to her after.

Larry called the meeting to order and they went through the usual introductions and readings. Then Larry opened the floor for discussion. His old history teacher said he'd gone to his family reunion after all after they'd dropped most of the events specifically involving alcohol. "Apparently I wasn't the only family member to object to all the drinking opportunities."

"Who objected? The others in recovery?" Ross teased.

"No, the Baptist deacons."

They all laughed. Other members spoke up with minor concerns. Ross admitted he didn't think he was getting anywhere with Emma. "She continues to act like I'm not there and her uncle is still giving me the death glare."

"Oh, no. Please tell us you're not giving up," Miss Loraine fretted.

"No, I'm hanging in there. I told my boss at the feed store we had to work around the theater. He's agreed to let me go a little early on Friday afternoons."

"What about making our meetings?" Larry asked.

"Saturdays I work seven to one."

Miranda looked up. "Then you come here and on to the theater? That's brutal."

"I can do it," he stated and puffed out his chest. "I'm not that old."

"Never said you were," she mumbled.

Melanie took her turn and Miranda sank back into silence. She was every bit as quiet and distracted today as she had been last night. Maybe even more so. He was still navigating the waters of recovery, but even he knew that bottling things up could send the most secure in their sobriety right back to the bottle.

Miranda was the last person he'd want that to happen to.

They had gone around the circle and those who'd volunteered had spoken. Larry looked around the group. "Would anyone else like to talk about their week?" His gaze landed across the circle at Miranda. "Anyone?" he prompted softly.

"This week sucked," Miranda said quietly. "Big time."

"How so?" Larry asked. "Would you like to talk about it?"

Miranda's shoulders twitched. "May as well. I tried to talk to Emma and couldn't get through to her. I talked to her about forgiving Ross but she's not buying it. It's eating her alive, but she won't admit it. She's got a wall around herself a mile high about him and I couldn't find the words to get over it."

Ross started. She'd tried to talk to Emma on his behalf? Was that what had her so morose? A conversation that didn't go well? That didn't sound like the Miranda he knew.

"Oh, dear, that must have been a disappointment," Miss Loraine soothed. "As close as you are to the girl."

He didn't realize Miranda and his daughter were all that close. He should've known.

"Disappointment doesn't begin to describe it." She took a breath. "I've gotten really close to her since her mother died and her father, well, you know…" She trailed off helplessly.

"Say it. I fell even deeper in the bottle, and then I left," Ross said. "After embarrassing the life out of her in front of everyone at the Durango."

"Well, yes," Miranda sighed. "Anyway, I made myself available to her when she needed someone and she turned to me. It's good for me, and I'd like to think it's good for her."

"I'm sure it's good for her," Adam said. "Especially with her mother gone, having you, her mother's best friend to turn to." He looked at her with compassion. "I can see where it would be good for you too, as close as she was to Tommy. Everyone at the funeral lost it when she put those flowers on his casket."

Ross could see tears in Miranda's eyes. "She was the only one of his little friends who stuck by him until the end. The bald head, the bloating, the wires coming out of him—they never seemed to bother her. To her he was always her best friend, Tommy. I'll always love her for it." She thumbed a tear out of her eye. "He would've turned twenty this coming Thursday."

Ross nodded to himself. *Now he got it.* She was mourning her dead son, and not getting through to Emma exacerbated the loss.

"How are you doing?" Miss Loraine asked quietly. "Is it getting to you?"

"You mean do I want to stop by the liquor store and get a big box of Pino Grigio and drink away the pain? You better believe it."

The group erupted with a chorus of "No" and "Please don't."

"Miranda, you don't want to do that," Larry said. "You've worked too hard and stayed sober too long."

"I didn't say I was going to. I said I wanted to," she groused.

But he wondered how easy it would be for wanting to to become going to, especially with the kind of anguish she was bound to be feeling. As much as he hated his estrangement from Emma, at least his child was alive, breathing, and thriving.

Miranda's boy was in a box in the ground.

Larry extracted a promise from her that she would call him if the temptation became too great and the conversation moved on.

They adjourned a half-hour or so later and Miranda went to her car before anyone had the chance to speak to her. Ross spent a few minutes chatting with the group and drinking another cup of coffee. He was pleased and surprised when a couple of the men invited him to join them for breakfast at the café in Devine Monday morning before he went to work. Nothing AA related, merely breakfast and some company. A welcome change from the ongoing disappointment from the continued cold shoulder at the Durango.

He accepted their invitation with pleasure.

***

Miranda's car was already in the Durango lot when he pulled in. He didn't feel like making the block, so he took his chances and went through the back. Miranda was standing beside the light and sound console and didn't look up when he walked by. Josh snagged him the minute he walked into the lobby to sort tickets and paperclip them together by party so they could be picked up more easily. It was a mindless exercise, which gave him time to think about Miranda and wonder if he had any business getting involved with the issues she was facing this week.

Which didn't make much sense, he admitted to himself as he clipped the last of the tickets together and reported to the t-shirt counter. He'd been ready to reach out to her, but that was before he learned why Miranda was not herself. Before he'd found out how close she'd become to his daughter. How important they were to one another.

The last thing he wanted to do was fuck with a relationship which meant so much to them. If he got in any deeper with Miranda, Emma was bound to find out. It could wreck Miranda's relationship with his girl and trash any chance of a reconciliation. Yet, at the same time, he was worried about Miranda tonight. The last thing she needed was the box of Pino Grigio that was tempting her so badly.

He didn't know what the hell to do.

Chapter Eight

Ross

Ross was on autopilot for most of the evening, selling tees and restocking the concession stand, for once oblivious to whatever Kevin and Emma were doing. He made quick work of counting the money with Josh and ducked out. He was still debating the wisdom of his involvement when he took the exit and barreled down the farm to the market road leading to the ranch. He'd about decided to let Miranda sort things out on her own when he drove past her ranch and spotted her car parked by the family cemetery. He slammed on the brakes and made the turn into the Bar T, hoping to god she wasn't sitting beside Tommy's grave tying one on like he'd done at Renee's more times than he could count.

He bounced down the rutted drive and parked his truck beside her car. He got out his phone to use as a flashlight and pushed open the gate. Dressed in her signature backstage black, he had to search for a minute until he spotted her sitting cross-legged on the ground in the back, her elbows on her knees and her head in her hands. There didn't appear to be a bottle or a box or a cup, so she'd at least for forgone the temptation to drink. But from the quiet crying blending with the sigh of the hot night wind in the leaves, she was far from all right.

He aimed the flashlight down and picked his way over a gravel path past old gravestones and piles of dried leaves to where she sat on the ground, leaning against Tommy's sparkling white headstone. His footsteps crunched in the gravel and she looked up with tears streaming down her face. "I miss him. I miss my baby so much." She buried her face in her hands and sobbed.

Her pain lanced through him. “I know you miss him.” He sank down to the ground beside her and took her in his arms, crooning softly as she cried. He couldn’t imagine her pain. Losing a wife had been heart-wrenching enough. But to lose a child would have to be the most devastating thing ever. Having an asshole husband walk out when the going got tough, it was no wonder she’d fallen into the bottle.

She cried for long minutes as the pain poured forth. He rocked her back and forth, holding her gently as sobs shook her body. When her crying subsided, she looked up with tear-stained cheeks she said brokenly. “He would have been twenty next Thursday.”

“That’s what you said this afternoon.” He twisted around so he was facing her. “Emma turned twenty in June.”

“They were in the same class at school.”

“I remember.”

“They were with one another all the time on weekends and in the summer. Sometimes here and sometimes at your place. They raised such a fuss at being apart it was easier to let them be together. Renee said Emma really missed him after he died.”

“We both dried plenty of her tears that fall. I’ve often wondered why they were so close.”

“Renee thought it was because they were both only children.”

“Only and lonely.” Ross shifted to a more comfortable position. “Which in our case wasn’t by choice. We tried for years but it never happened again for us.”

“We were going to try for another when Tommy got cancer. Tom said he wasn’t risking another sick kid, and then he left.” She wiped the tears off her face.

“Did you ever consider having another child?”

“Not really. It all went to hell after Tommy died. By the time I sobered up I was already well into my thirties. I’d spent the last two years of Tommy’s life as a single parent, and as much as I would have loved another baby, I didn’t think a recovering alcoholic had any business raising a child alone, although some pull it off beautifully.”

“You probably could’ve managed.”

“But it would’ve been unfair as hell to a child if I couldn’t. I was scared to try.” She took a breath. “I’m left with my memories and can only wonder what might have been had Tommy lived. Memories that break my heart and make me cry every January and August. The month he died and the month he was born."

"What about marrying again? Having a child with a good man? Did you consider that?"

"I wouldn't have been averse to the idea, but nobody ever came along," she said frankly. "Now, even if I did find someone, I'd be too old."

"Really? Kevin's wife had one last year. She's at least your age."

Miranda snorted. "Letti's crazy as a road lizard. Plus, she's married to a man fifteen years her junior who wanted kids. A husband her age probably wouldn't be so keen. You're my age. Think about it. Would you want to start over at this point?"

Ross recoiled in horror at the thought. "Night feedings? Teething? Potty training? God spare me." He reached out and took her hand. "I'm glad you and Emma have found your way to one another."

"So am I. It helps."

"I know something else that might help. You said Tommy would've been twenty this coming Thursday. We need to go out and celebrate."

Miranda eyes widened and she blinked rapidly like her lids were sputtering. "*Celebrate?* Why in the hell would I want to do that? He's dead. There's nothing to celebrate."

"Miranda, there most certainly is something to celebrate. A child's life. A life that ended way too damn soon, but nevertheless was lived. Tommy's life needs to be acknowledged. It needs to be remembered and honored. *He* needs to be remembered and honored. What better way than to celebrate on his birthday?"

"I don't know. It seems weird." Miranda looked at him doubtfully. "I never heard of anybody doing something like that."

"You never heard of *Dia de los Muertos*? Day of the Dead? That's when a lot of people celebrate the lives of their dead family. Their ancestors. This wouldn't be so different." He smiled. "Only instead of decorating his headstone, we'll go to his favorite restaurant, eat food he loved, and have cake and balloons. You share your favorite memories. We talk about him and remember the good times. Your son deserves to be remembered, so let's do that."

They sat quietly while she seemed to be thinking about it. “He liked plain white cake the best. With buttercream frosting,” she whispered.

“Like they make at Lola’s bakery?”

“Yes. Like hers. I had them make one every year.”

“So we get Lola to make him a buttercream cake. What else?”

“He loved chicken fingers and mac and cheese. He ate that sometimes when he was too sick to eat anything else.”

“Okay. Chicken fingers and mac and cheese it is. Where did he like to eat?”

“He loved the cafeteria on Southeast Military. I took him there a lot.”

“So we get our chicken fingers and mac and cheese at the cafeteria.”

“And he loved red balloons. I’d take them to him in the hospital. No matter how badly he felt, they always made him smile.”

“Red balloons, coming up. Anything else?”

She was silent for a minute. “I don’t think so.”

“All right, then.” He got out his phone and Googled the cafeteria. “They close at eight, so we need to be there by seven. Can I pick you up at six, or do you want to meet me there?”

She looked at him doubtfully. “You really think we should celebrate?”

“Absolutely.” He took Miranda’s hand. “You’re gonna have him on your mind anyway. What’s better? Sitting by yourself crying and jonesing for booze, or eating mac and cheese and remembering the fun times you had with a wonderful kid?”

“Maybe you’re right. I can get out of there early on Thursday if you want to pick me up here.”

“Atta girl.” He gave her hand a squeeze. “Now, my ass is getting tired of this hard ground and yours is bound to be as well. Whattaya say we get on home to our late-night snacks?”

“Sounds like a plan.”

He helped her up and they walked hand in hand to the cemetery gate. “Are you gonna be all right now?” he asked as she pushed the gate shut behind them.

“I’ll be fine. Thanks.”

She got in her car and headed down the rutted drive to her old farmhouse. He headed back toward the highway and his farm. He made a mental checklist of things to accomplish before Thursday. Order and pick up the cake from Lola's. Order red balloons from the party store. Make sure the cafeteria was serving mac and cheese and chicken fingers on Thursday evening. Take a nice shirt and his best jeans to the laundry and arrange for them to be ready by Thursday. Find a dance club near the cafeteria where they could listen to music and do a little dancing. Change the sheets on his bed and find one of those scented candles women seemed to love.

Wait. *Wait.* Clothes to the laundry? A dance club? No. Clean sheets and a candle? Hell, no. He didn't know what in god's name he was thinking. This was supposed to be about Miranda's state of mind. About helping her snap out of her funk. About her continuing sobriety. It wasn't supposed to be about looking good or holding her close on the dance floor or having her body intimately intwined with his on clean sheets in the candlelight. It wasn't supposed to be a fucking date.

Or a sleepover.

Or a booty call.

It wasn't about getting naked with Miranda, as badly as he wanted to.

If he kept telling himself to rein it in, he might start to believe he could.

***

Miranda

Miranda smoothed down the front of her dress and looked at herself in the full-length mirror. She turned from side to side. Crapola. It looked like she's been melted and poured into the damn thing. She stripped it off and swore when she looked at the tag. It was supposedly her size. But she hadn't gone dress shopping in ages. Not since she'd sobered up and started eating healthy again. She'd gained the twenty or so pounds recovering alcoholics routinely put on. Great for their health, especially if they'd been drinking too many of their dinners. Not so great for their wardrobes.

She rifled through the rest of her dresses and swore again. Not one of them was going to fit. Which was craptastic in the extreme. The rest of her wardrobe was limited to clothes she wore to the

Durango. She went through her slacks and pulled out the nicest ones she owned, which were well cut and looked good on her. Now for a top. She made a quick foray into those and was about to give up and wear a black blouse when she came across the beautiful cherry red sparkly knit top Renee had given her the last Christmas before the wreck. She'd loved it at the time but hadn't ever worn it, had never even tried it on. The red would show if she were backstage during scene changes and it had been pushed to the back of the closet and forgotten. Maybe it would look good tonight. She shook out the wrinkles and held it up to her. Oh, yes. If it fit, it most certainly would suit.

She made quick work of the tags and pulled it over her head and stared at herself in the mirror. Thank god. The top fit perfectly, clinging to her curves and displaying an enticing bit of cleavage. The deep black slacks set it off to perfection. She studied herself in the mirror. Hmm. The outfit worked but at the same time lacked that special something that would take it up a notch from good to great. Over the years at the theater, she'd paid attention to Vivi Abonce and other fashion-conscious women who graced the stage or filled the audience. From them she'd learned there was a difference between looking good and looking awesome. She needed to do something to take it up that last notch to something special.

Tonight she wanted to look wonderful for Tommy, she told herself while she pawed through her accessories' drawer and her jewelry box. She wanted to look good for his birthday. She wanted to look special to celebrate his life.

Wanting to look good for Ross Ellis had nothing to do with it.

Yeah, right.

It didn't matter all that much why she wanted to look good. It beat sitting by herself thinking about the aching void in her life, the hollow emptiness nothing ever really filled. Sure, she'd thought of Tommy today. But somehow it wasn't getting to her the way it usually did. She'd had something else to think about. Of course it was all superficial. Clothes and makeup and looking good tonight weren't earth-shaking. But they were something else to think about besides the bone-numbing grief that would have been her companion otherwise.

She owed Ross a big one.

Miranda unearthed a sleek, modern necklace of multicolored cubes and crystals, another of Renee's gifts over the years. It might do the trick. She fastened the necklace and slipped in coordinating multicolored studs. Her freshly washed hair hung loose over her shoulders and down her back in a riot of curls. She'd almost bought a bottle of rinse to cover the encroaching gray but took another look and instead bought shampoo that brought out the silver highlights. The same trip to the drugstore had netted a few basic cosmetics to replace the dried-out specimens in her makeup kit, and tonight a little foundation, a bit of eyeshadow and mascara, and a deep rose red gloss on her lips graced her face. She dabbed on a bit of blush and was sliding into a pair of low-heeled dress shoes when she heard Ross's truck coming up the drive. She took one more look at herself in the mirror. She was not the beauty Renee had been. But she'd do.

A part of her wondered what Ross would think. Another part of her swore she didn't care.

She came down the stairs and opened the door as he crossed the front porch. In one hand he carried a box from Lola's and a grocery sack and the other was fisted around a bouquet of balloons. She smiled in delight. "Cake. Ice cream. Balloons! You remembered."

Ross smiled down at her. "Of course I remembered. And we have chicken fingers and mac and cheese coming up. Where do you want the cake?"

"Let's put it in the kitchen."

She took the cake box from him and carried it out to the large farmhouse kitchen. He followed her with the balloons. "Where do you want these?"

She looked around. "We can tie them to the back of the chairs. Tommy used to love to do that."

They tied a balloon to each of the kitchen chairs. "Can I get you something to drink?" she asked. "I have tea, fancy water and sodas in the fridge. Or I can make you a cup of coffee."

"Nah, I'm good. I've had I don't know how much coffee already today."

"Is that your go-to drink now?"

"It is. The coffee growers in South America celebrate the day I went into rehab. What's yours?"

"Oddly enough, fruit juices. The exotic kind, and the fancy water I offered. Piss-poor substitutes. All of them."

He snorted out a laugh. "I know what you mean." His eyes softened as he looked at her. "Let me tell you how pretty you look tonight."

"Thanks." *He noticed.* She felt a blush creep up her face. "You clean up nice yourself." He was wearing a crisply pressed dress shirt paired with starched black jeans she doubted he'd ironed himself, and a pair of black alligator boots Renee had given him for Christmas a few years back. From the way he filled out the shirt and jeans he appeared to be gaining back a little more of the weight he'd dropped. He looked good. Good enough to eat.

Good enough to back up against the wall and kiss the life out of.

Not going there, Miranda.

He ushered her out to his truck, freshly washed for the occasion. She noted with amusement he'd cleaned out the inside and taped up the split in the seat. He glanced over at her as he pulled onto the highway. "So how was your week?" he asked.

"You want the truth or a social lie?"

His face fell. "Bad?"

"Not bad like you're thinking. More along the lines of interesting. Entertaining, almost."

His eyebrow shot up. "How so?"

"Let's say nobody's been in a good mood. Maggie Gutierrez, our developmental director, spent the week pissed off because she had three big grants fall through, one of which her boyfriend had practically guaranteed the Durango would get. Cameron's upset because ticket sales are down and Josh thinks Cam blames him for it, and Josh and Rachel had a screaming match over whether to include *Oh! Calcutta!* in next year's lineup. Kevin's cranky because he made the mistake of teasing Letti about needing bifocals and she banished him to the guest room. Oh, and our set designer quit and left us high and dry for the next production." She snickered. "This was one week when all the drama definitely wasn't on the stage."

"Sounds like they're a bunch of drama queens to me."

"I wouldn't call them drama queens. But remember, we have an entire theater full of artistic, enormously creative people whose emotions run high and close to the surface. Then you throw in professional pride and artistic differences and it does get noisy on occasion."

He glanced over at her. "You ever get involved?"

"Oh, hell yes. My brutal honesty has bitten me in the ass more than once. Letti didn't speak to me for a week when I told her she was too old to play an ingenue. She wasn't too happy with me when I seconded Jessica's decision to cast Emma as Ariel in *The Little Mermaid.* She was determined that role to go to her daughter."

Ross's face fell. "I wish I'd seen her in it."

"You never went?" Miranda asked.

Ross sighed. "One of the many sins I'm trying to make amends for. Was she good?"

"Absolutely wonderful."

He smacked the steering wheel with his palm. "I have so many fucking regrets it's not funny. So much I'd do differently if I had the chance."

"Regrets are a waste of time. The only direction any of us can go at this point is forward. Which you are doing. So chill. Tell me about your week. Do you like working at the feed store?"

He did, and he regaled her all the way to San Antonio with funny stories about past and present customers and their many foibles. The cafeteria parking lot was almost full and there was a line out the door. "Everyone had the same idea we did," Miranda said as they took their place in line.

"Everyone's tired of being cooped up. It's like we've all been let out of jail."

Her face fell as a memory washed over her. "Tommy used to get so impatient in line. I had to make up little games to keep him occupied."

"Difference between boys and girls, I guess. Emma was always patient. What kinds of games did you make up?"

"Stuff like patty-cake when he was really little. If a highchair was available, I'd grab one and magically produce a couple pieces of paper and a crayon. Tom would push the highchair through the line and I'd juggle both trays. By the time Tom left, Tommy was big enough to handle his own tray. Until he got so weak and was in a wheelchair." She stopped and took a breath. "But we came anyway. I was determined he'd live life to the very end. I'm proud to say he did."

"What else did he like to do besides come here? Did he like any other restaurants?"

"He did. He loved Arturo's in Pleasanton, and the other Mexican place in Jourdanton. For some reason Mexican tasted funny to him when he was on chemo, so when he'd go off we'd pig out on it, at least until he went back on."

The line inched forward. "What else did he like to do?"

"He loved to ride. The last Christmas he was healthy, Tom splurged and bought Rosie."

"The little roan mare."

"The mare. Anyway, he rode almost every day until he got sick, and as often as he could after. I had to ride with him, but he was up on her for the last time four days before he died."

"Where's Rosie now? Do you still own her?"

"No. She needed more love and attention than I could give her. She was still young enough to train, so I donated her in Tommy's name to an equine therapy organization. She spends her days giving rides to special needs children. The therapists say she's one of their best horses. Sometimes I think she learned a lot when Tommy was sick."

"Of course she did."

Ross asked her a few more questions as the line moved closer to the entryway. They finally reached the steam table and they each got a tray. Miranda peered down at the entrée selection. "Oops. No chicken fingers tonight. That's okay. Tommy liked fish too." She hoped her disappointment didn't show too much.

"Guess again." Ross asked the salad server if she would get the manager. The manager appeared a couple of minutes later. "I called about chicken fingers and mac and cheese. You have those plates ready for us?"

"I do, sir."

The manager disappeared and came back a couple of minutes later with two plates heaping with chicken fingers and generous helpings of mac and cheese. "Here you go. Is there anything else we can help you with?" the man asked.

"No, this will definitely do it. Thanks so much."

The manager smiled at them. "You're more than welcome. Enjoy your celebration."

Miranda felt tears prickle her eyes as she took the overflowing plate. "It's what he liked," she said. "Thanks."

"You're welcome."

"How'd you know they weren't on the menu tonight?"

"I called ahead. When I told them it was for a special occasion, the manager was more than happy to have some made."

"Thanks again. It makes tonight really special."

"Glad to oblige."

Miranda marveled at Ross's thoughtfulness. It was a quality that must've come with maturity and sobriety. She wondered how many other positive qualities the older, sober Ross had developed.

Ross paid for their meals and they found a booth in the back along the wall. They were quiet for a few minutes while they tucked into their dinner. To her surprise and Ross's amusement, she killed the entire plate. She looked down at the empty dish sheepishly. "I guess I was hungry."

Ross's lips twitched. "That would appear to be the case." He looked down at his empty plate. "I guess I was hungry as well."

"Guess you were. It reminds me of the times Renee and I brought Tommy and Emma here. We'd buy one plate for them to split and there would still be leftovers. Emma loved the chicken fingers as much as Tommy did. The mac and cheese, not so much. She'd eat it to be nice to him."

"She was a sweet kid that way."

Miranda nodded. "Still is. She mentored the younger Academy students while she was still in the Academy herself. She does even more with them now."

Ross looked at her with an expression she couldn't quite understand. "How invested is she in the acting? How serious is she about it?"

"Serious about it? No more or less than any of our other actors. She does the best job she knows how when she's up on the stage."

"No. I mean, is she studying it in college? Is she planning a career in it? Kevin tried, you know. Ran off to Hollywood for several years. Is she gonna do that?" His façade slipped and he looked at her anxiously.

How sad. He and Emma were so far estranged that he didn't know her major.

"You mean, is she running off to California like he did? I seriously doubt it. She's a pre-law major, and we've got plenty of law schools here in Texas."

"Thank god." He relaxed visibly. "If she went off to California I really wouldn't ever have a chance with her. Seems she's not doing anything with the drama."

"Oh, I wouldn't say that. She'll use it in a court of law, just like Kevin will."

"I guess so. It really doesn't surprise me, her wanting to go into law. She used to play courtroom when she was a little kid. She'd be the lawyer. She'd line up her dolls to be on the jury and Tommy was her judge."

"I remember that," Miranda said eagerly. "That poor old Raggedy Andy got convicted every time. They'd play courtroom when it rained. When the weather was good they'd be playing farmer outside. That was Tommy's favorite game."

"Renee got lots of weeds out of the garden that way," Ross snickered.

"So did I."

They laughed. "Emma loved the water when she was little," he went on. "We used to take her to the Summersets' lake condo for the weekend. She was fearless in the water. We had to watch her like a hawk."

"Renee and I had 'em both swimming by the time they were two. Something else they loved to do together—swim in the stock tank or down by the creek. I always felt for city kids. No swimming holes for them. They have to make do in a pool full of chlorine."

"Poor little city babies." Ross mocked a sad face. "Remember the time they tried to take that old cow dog of mine swimming with them? Buster wasn't amused."

Miranda laughed. Buster hadn't been amused in the least.

And so the conversation went. She would think of some memory of Tommy, or he would remember something about Emma, or they would recall something involving both kids. Miranda felt the knot of grief within her start to unravel as they remembered a happier time. While they were reminiscing, she felt herself drawn to the man sitting across from her as he shared his memories and listened to hers. Gone was the out-of-control drunk who'd been so awful to his daughter at the theater. Gone was the dead-eyed man she'd ordered out of the balcony. In his place sat a warm, sweet, thoughtful man who'd gone out of his way to help her cope with her sorrow, and who'd taken a day of heartbreak and made it into a time of warm remembrance.

If things had been different, this was a man she could get into. Big time.

But they had no business getting together. It would be a bad idea all around. For so many reasons. Which sucked. Big time.

It was a crying shame things were the way they were.

They lingered over cups of coffee until it was closing time. Ross took her hand as they walked to the truck. His touch was warm and intimate, sending chills up her arm. "Would you like to go somewhere and listen to a bit of music? Maybe even do a little dancing?" he asked offhandedly as he unlocked the truck.

Whoa. She hadn't been expecting that. They'd been relating to one another as friends tonight. Other than complimenting her on her appearance, he'd given no indication he even thought of her as anything more. He sure hadn't seemed interested in anything else. But maybe he was. She glanced over at him. Underneath his supposed nonchalance, there was something there. Desire maybe. She wasn't quite sure what to label it, but she sure would like to find out what was behind his casual façade.

Maybe he was as interested as she was. Bad idea and all. Besides, doing a little dancing wasn't going to hurt anything. It wasn't like he'd invited her into his bed.

"Sure," she said, striving for the same nonchalance coming from him. "That would be nice. Anyplace in particular you're thinking?"

"What kind of music do you like?"

"I like all kinds, but if we're dancing it probably needs to be country. I can do that without stepping all over your feet."

"Country it is, then. I know a place not too far from here that might be fun."

Chapter Nine

Miranda

Ross pulled out of the parking lot and headed toward a part of town Miranda hadn't visited for a while. Her lips twitched when he pulled into a familiar parking lot. The place he knew was the most famous western dance hall in the city. She and every country kid for miles around grew up driving into San Antonio and sneaking in here on Saturday night, hoping their fake IDs would fool security. "Ever been here?" He winked.

"Oh, maybe once or twice. You?"

"A good part of my youth was misspent in here."

She looked at him doubtfully. "You think we'll be all right?" she asked. If ever a place was full of triggers, it would be a booze-soaked dance hall.

"We won't know 'til we try," he said with more optimism than she felt.

He took her by the hand and they trotted across the parking lot. The smell of bar food and beer hit her as they walked in the door.

Ross paid their cover and they found a table far away from the long, L-shaped bar along the wall to the right of the stage. A huge sawdust-dappled dance floor graced the center of the room with tables four or five deep lining it all the way to the walls. Miranda half-expected a DJ and Karaoke machine and was pleasantly surprised to see a band setting up. There were a few other couples scattered around the room and a handful of tables occupied by groups of college age kids who were already three sheets to the wind. But singles, couples, and small groups were drifting in a few at a time. By ten, the place would be packed.

By midnight, the crowd would be soused.

The thought made her uneasy. Even after all the years she'd been sober, the thought of joining them was too tempting.

She looked over at Ross. He was much newer in his sobriety than she was in hers. He seemed to be all right. Maybe his triggers weren't the same as hers. Maybe the smell of beer and whiskey didn't set him off the way it did her.

Or maybe he was faking it, not wanting to seem weak in front of her.

A bored-looking waitress in a tank top displaying a little too much cleavage walked over to the table. "Two for one beer until ten. Or the lady gets half off everything all evening." She flipped open her pad. "What'll it be?"

"A Coke for me," Miranda said.

"Dr. Pepper," Ross told the waitress.

The woman's brows went up as her lips pursed before she stalked off. "Oops. There went her big tip," Miranda said.

"I don't want to think of the money I dropped on big-boobed waitresses over the years. One of the hazards of being a drunk. What do lady drunks throw their money away on? Besides booze?"

"I can't speak for the rest, but I drank and Primed. You don't want to know how many piles of packages I'd find on my front porch."

"Ouch."

The server returned with their drinks and an insincere smile on her face. "Let me know if I can bring you anything else."

They thanked her, and Miranda glanced toward the stage as she sipped her Coke. "Looks like they're about set up."

"Good. I'm ready to dance. Hope you don't mind being the first couple on the dance floor."

"Don't mind a bit." Being first wasn't her thing, but from the way Ross was gripping his glass of soda, the atmosphere was getting to him as well. Coming here hadn't been the brightest idea for either of them, but she'd been thinking about spending a bit of time in Ross's arms, not about the temptation they were going to feel being in a bar.

They should've gone dancing in her living room.

But they were here. Ross had gone to the trouble and brought her, and it would be rude to suggest they leave. Besides, she wanted to be near him for at least a couple of dances, to feel his arms around her as they moved with the music. Presumably he wanted the same thing with her. They could last for a few dances without the temptation to drink overwhelming them.

They sipped their sodas and made idle conversation while the band tuned up and did sound checks. Then the young band leader stepped to the microphone and introduced the band. "We're starting off with 'It's Five o: clock Somewhere' by Alan Jackson." The band launched into the lively anthem advocating daytime drinking.

She and Ross looked at one another. "You have to be fucking kidding me," Ross said.

She jumped up and grabbed him by the hand. "I don't care what it's about. Let's take advantage of the music."

He followed her to the dance floor and took her in his arms. Sure enough, they were the first ones out, but the band leader knew what he was doing starting with a crowd pleaser and it wasn't long before the dance floor started filling up.

Ross's misspent youth served him well as he expertly guided her around the floor, their steps blending surprisingly well for two people who'd never danced together before. She was pleasantly winded, but by no means ready to sit down when the song ended and the band immediately segued into "Blame it on Your Heart" by Patti Loveless.

They kept dancing, not missing a beat through that one, and then Sara Evans' "Suds in the Bucket," and of all things, Blake Shelton's remake of "Footloose," which had them joining in a line dance populated by a group who'd memorized the steps from the movie.

Ross didn't miss a beat, although he looked a little relieved when the band leader announced they would be slowing down a bit for the next number. "All you fellas out there, grab your lady and make her glad she came with you tonight."

Ross opened his arms and she moved into them. The band launched into "Slow Dancing in the Parking Lot." Only they were slow dancing in a funky old dance hall with sawdust on the floor, and beer and whiskey flowing freely.

Ross drew her close, his body warm and a little sweaty next to hers, his arm firm around his waist and her hand on his shoulder. His chest was muscular beneath the starched white shirt, his body hard and more filled out than it had been when she kissed him last month.

They moved slowly to the music, not doing too much more than swaying together. And that was fine with her. It was heaven having a man this close, but it wasn't just any man. It was Ross next to her, strong and masculine, whose nearness was turning her on and making her want to do things she hadn't wanted to do in quite some time.

It wasn't as though she'd been celibate over the years. She'd had plenty of one-night stands during her drinking days, and had gotten as far as booty calls with a handful after she'd gone sober, but not one of them had turned her on like this. Made her nipples stiffen or her panties wet during one slow dance.

Ross turned her on like no man had since Tom, and maybe even more than he had.

That was saying a lot.

They moved slowly to the music their bodies plastered together. The band switched effortlessly to "I Don't Want to Miss a Thing." Aerosmith from a country band? She didn't care what they played, as long as she could stay in Ross's arms.

They danced two more dances. Then the band launched into the old George Strait "I Cross my Heart" and they both stiffened. That was the song the band played for the bridal dance at Ross and Renee's wedding. Miranda took Ross by the hand and led him off the dance floor. "I'm ready for another soda," she said lightly.

Ross signaled for the waitress. After she grudgingly brought them more sodas, Ross was clutching his glass even tighter than before, and the sound of the increasingly raucous crowd was beginning to crawl up Miranda's back. Ross nodded quickly when she suggested they leave.

They collapsed into the truck and looked at one another. "I'm sorry," he said as he stared at the front of the honky-tonk. "I had no idea how hard it would be. Going in there and not drinking."

"I should have. I've had a lot more practice being a sober alcoholic than you have. If I'd been thinking I would've said we could dance in my living room. Lots less temptation there."

"I don't know about that."

She glanced over at him. Damn, it was too dark in the truck to see much, but it looked to her like he was blushing. She reached over and placed her hand on his leg. "You might be right."

He grinned wickedly and it was her turn to blush.

They rode back without talking much. Delicious chills ran up and down Miranda's spine. She had no idea what was going to happen once they got to her place. Maybe they would do the wise thing, ignore the attraction, and eat cake before Ross went home. Maybe they'd dance a little more before she sent Ross home.

And maybe they would give in to what they were both feeling tonight, as stupid as that would be.

God help her, she was going for stupid.

Ross pulled into the entrance to her ranch, and the truck bounced up the rutted drive to her house. He followed her inside and they stared at one another for a moment in the entry. He made no move toward her, and Miranda wondered if she'd imagined his interest earlier.

Disappointing. But she could live with it.

She made herself smile as she reached for his hand. "C'mon to the kitchen. There's a cake in there I'm dying to cut."

He nodded and followed her through the house. "You ready for that coffee now?" she asked.

"Sounds good."

She put a coffee pod in the coffeemaker. Together they got out plates and forks and she fished a bottle of flavored water from the fridge. He retrieved his coffee while she cut two generous pieces of cake and added scoops of ice cream. He sat down across from her at her old kitchen table, scarred from three generations of use, and forked up a bite. "Damn, I'd forgotten how good Lola's can make a cake."

She took a bite of hers and moaned. "You're right. It's been years since I had one of her cakes. Maybe I could take one to AA sometime."

"You can take the rest of this one if you'd like."

"Nuh-uh. No way. You and I are gonna eat every bite of this puppy."

They polished off their first pieces of cake and second ones as well. She looked across the table. Ross was staring at her intensely. She swallowed. It hadn't been her imagination. His expression held more than mere interest. There was desire in his eyes. But there was wariness as well. Wariness and uncertainty. He wanted her as badly as she wanted him, and he was every bit as hesitant as she was.

Smart man.

She covered the leftover cake and put the dishes in the sink. She turned around to find him standing right behind her. "You promised me a dance or two in your living room. I'm gonna collect those dances."

She nodded. He took her by the hand and headed to the living room. He fiddled with his phone for a minute before smiling mysteriously. "I'll put it on speaker." He hit the screen a couple of times and *"Lady in Red"* started playing. "I thought of this song when I saw you tonight," he said as he held out his arms to her.

Wordlessly she melted into him. They circled the living room, clinging to one another as the haunting lyrics filled the room. The delicious chills returned, even more intensely than in the crowded dance hall, their bodies plastered tightly together. Miranda was achingly aware of Ross's warm, hard body next to hers, the scent of his soap and aftershave and the essence that was him. She squashed down her doubts. She shoved her common sense to one side. All she cared about was: she desired this man. She needed him in her bed, in her body, in every way she could have him. She needed him tonight.

Tomorrow could take care of itself.

The song ended and immediately Eric Clapton's "Wonderful Tonight" came on. Miranda smiled as she buried her face in his neck. She loved anthems to beautiful women, although they hardly applied to her. As the music stopped, Ross framed her face between his hands and dipped his head. "I've got to kiss you. I've dreamed of kissing you again more times than I can count."

He lowered his head. Their lips met in an explosion of heat and lust and desire. Miranda wrapped her arms around his waist as his cradled her backside. They pulled one another impossibly close. His chest was warm against hers and the evidence of his desire swelled against her thigh. Her heart pounded in her ears and her breathing hitched as her desire for him grew. The past, his drinking, her drinking, Renee's death, his resentments, none of it mattered. All that really, truly mattered was she wanted him in her bed tonight.

And, it seemed, he wanted her just as desperately.

They kissed and touched as their tongues danced a pleasurable duel for long minutes. When Ross lifted his head and stared into her eyes, he said, "I want you. I want you in my bed. I changed the sheets and put out candles. Even got some condoms. Just in case."

"My bed's closer. My sheets are fresh, and there would be a brand-new candle sitting on the nightstand. I have condoms. A whole box. Just in case."

"A whole box, huh?" His eyes danced.

"I'm an optimist." She stared at him. "You know this is foolish, right? We have no business doing this."

"Ask me if I give a shit. Are you worried?"

"At the moment, no."

"Then what are we waiting for?" He swept her into his arms. "Up those stairs, I presume."

She nodded and he started up the stairs with her in his arms.

Chapter Ten

Miranda

Ross strode down the hall carrying her. "Which room?"

"The one on the end." She pointed out the bedroom at the end of the hall, dimly lit by a small nightlight she always left burning. Miranda had deliberately left the blinds open and the windows were filled with the gentle glow of starlight. He carried her to the nearest window and eased her down, holding her close. "This is beautiful. I never realized there were so many windows up here."

"My great-greats who built the house loved the outdoors. Every room up here is like this." She lit the candle on the nightstand, the flickering flame lighting the room in a soft glow.

"Beautiful view. But the one beside me is every bit as lovely." He bent his head for another kiss, this one hard and quick. His hands trembled as he fingered the edge of her sweater. "The top is beautiful, but it has to go." He whipped the sweater over her head and gazed at her breasts, visible beneath her lacy bra.

She stiffened, suddenly paralyzed by shyness. She hadn't thought this through. With the weight she'd put on, she was hardly the shapely girl she'd been in her twenties. Compared to the slim, beautiful woman he'd been married to, she felt lumpy. "What's the matter?" he asked softly. "Second thoughts about screwing the neighborhood drunk?"

"No. Second thoughts about taking off my clothes in front of the sexiest man to come my way in a long time. Maybe we should blow out the candle."

"Why would we want to do that?"

She sat down on the edge of the bed. "I'm not in the shape I used to be in."

He sighed and sat down beside her. “I looked up those two songs to say for me what I didn’t know how to come out and say myself. Miranda, you’re rockin’ it. You always have and you sure as hell still do. You’re carrying more weight than you used to, but so what? It all went to the right places.” He gestured to her lace-covered breasts. “Gorgeous. Jesus, girl, didn’t you feel how hard you’re making my cock? I want to lay a few more kisses on your sexy mouth before I take the Miranda tour and kiss every inch of your delectable body. I’ve daydreamed about doing this too damned many times to count.”

“You have?”

“Damned right. I almost put the tractor in the ditch last week imagining you with your clothes off. So can we please get on with it before I lose my nerve?”

Miranda blinked. He was as insecure as she was.

Somehow, knowing that made it easier.

She stood and shimmied out of her slacks, kicking her shoes across the room and standing in front of him in nothing but her lacy panties and bra. His breath hitched as he jerked off his boots and socks and shed his jeans and shirt. His tee went flying and his boxer briefs disappeared, leaving him naked in front of her. Miranda swallowed as she unhooked the bra and tossed it on the floor. Her panties went next, leaving her as bare as he was.

They stared at one another in the candlelight. Ross without his clothes was a sight to behold. While he had a few pounds to go before he’d be up to his healthiest weight, his body was hard and strong. His shoulders and arms were muscled from years of outdoor work. His chest was broad and generously sprinkled with chestnut hair, which tapered a sexy trail down between his washboard abs and flared again around his jutting cock. His thighs were muscled, strong, and hard. He didn’t have the body of a twenty-year-old. At forty-two he wasn’t going to. But he was a fine specimen just the same. She could hardly wait to get her hands on him. Kiss and touch him, and feel him inside her. Her nipples pebbled and she felt dampness rush between her legs.

If looking at Ross was this big a turn on, no telling what having sex with him was going to be like.

He reached out and touched her beaded nipple with his finger. “For me?”

"For you."

"Then let me thank you for that." Gently, he laid her on the bed and followed her there, leaning down and taking her nipple in his mouth. A stab of desire shot through her body, and she nearly came up off the bed. "Good lord, woman, you pack a punch," he murmured as he moved to the other nipple and gave it the same treatment.

She reached for him, but he pushed her down into the covers. "Nope. This is for you. I'll get my turn later."

Then he began an assault on her senses she'd never expected in her wildest dreams. His lips and his fingers were everywhere: on her lips, her neck, her breasts, and then her stomach. His touch was hot and tantalizing, setting her body on fire as she trembled. Her muscles clenched and she felt herself begin to tingle. His fingers drifted lower, crossing the triangle of hair and exploring her intimately. He seemed to be in no hurry, paying homage to her body as no one had in a long time, if ever. She reveled in every touch, every stroke, as he found the core of her desire and caressed it, teasing it into a hard nub of need and want. She moaned as his fingers persisted in their sensual assault, her body growing taut as he drew her closer and closer to the edge. "Ross, I—" She cried out as she toppled over the cliff, tremors shaking her body as a sharp, hard orgasm engulfed her. Wave after wave tore through her as she gave herself up to the sheer delight of it.

Ross rested his hand on her thigh as the tremors slowly subsided. "Been awhile?" he asked softly.

"Too damn long. Except for Valentino. He's a great lover until the power goes out."

Ross laughed. "Maybe you should try Vladimir. He's cordless." He scooted down and gently pushed open her legs. "Let me in here. I've got Valentino and Vladimir both beat. I want all of you."

He nuzzled her thighs and kissed his way up her legs until he was at her sweet spot again. Then he returned to his sensual assault. Only this time it was his lips turning her boneless, as his tongue took the place of his fingers, drawing her back into a sensual vortex with only a few touches and caresses.

She let herself lay back and savor the sensations washing over her as her body again soared, roaring to a second climax even harder than the first. "Damn, that was awesome," she breathed as the last of the tremors shook her. She fumbled for the condom box and handed him a foil packet. "Here. I want you inside me for the next one."

"Delighted to oblige." He rolled on the condom with trembling fingers and moved between her legs.

He entered her slowly at first, but when he saw she was ready for him, he thrust his cock in all the way, moving with her in a rhythm that had her climbing again. Only this time he was climbing with her as they moved faster and their desire ramped up until she felt yet another orgasm coming, and when she cried out he let himself go, groaning a as they climaxed together, tremors shaking them as they clung together for long minutes.

Still inside her, he rolled them so they were lying side by side. "One for the record books," he murmured as he looked into her eyes.

"Pretty much. It was wonderful. No, you were wonderful."

"You're pretty awesome yourself."

"And are about to be again, if it's not my imagination." He was swelling inside her.

"Maybe. Let me get rid of the condom."

He withdrew from her body and hopped off the bed, heading for the bathroom. He seemed totally unselfconscious in his nudity, his naked butt and back as gorgeous as the rest of him. Miranda watched with undisguised admiration as he came back to bed. His cock was already at half-mast and he looked at her with satisfaction and desire. "Up for another round?"

"My, you have a short recovery time." She pushed him down in the sheets. "Have you always been this quick on the draw?"

His face clouded. "Only when it's been three years since I've been with a woman."

Oops. Time to think about something else. "Tell you what. We're gonna take advantage of this phenomenon then, and I'm taking the Ross tour. That work for you?"

Without giving him a chance to respond, she snuggled down next to him. She wanted to explore every inch of his delectable body, to memorize his taste and the way he felt under her fingertips. His face, his neck, his chest, and his stomach were treated to her fingers and her lips as she made her way down his body.

Goose bumps broke out on his skin, and his cock swelled in response to her carnal exploration. Her fingers and her lips drifted further until she reached his cock. She gripped it in her palm, her firm touch making him harden even more. Then she bent down and took him into her mouth, enveloping the engorged tip. When he moaned and thrust up she took him deeper, as deeply as she could. He gasped and thrust as she used her lips and her tongue, bringing him almost to the brink, before he sat up and took her by the shoulders. "I want to finish inside you," he ground out. He lifted her up and was about to lower her when she gasped and pointed to the nightstand. "Damn. I forgot."

She leaned over and grabbed a condom, rolling it on before lowering herself onto him. This time she set the rhythm, the two of them moving together as again they spiraled toward the ultimate. She rode him hard, his hands on her hips as she guided them toward another explosive climax. She arched her back and called his name as tremors shook her body. He thrust into her as he too lost control, his cock jerking and trembling within her as he reached the pinnacle.

They trembled long minutes before she collapsed into his arms. "That was...that was—" She looked at him helplessly.

"I know. There really are no words." They lay together until he softened. She moved away and he disappeared into the bathroom.

Miranda rolled over and stared at the ceiling. At this point she had no idea what to expect. Would he want to spend the night, or would he put on his clothes and leave? The doubts she'd pushed aside earlier came roaring back. What they had done had been foolish in the extreme. Especially for him. He didn't yet have the twelve months of sobriety behind him that AA recommended before becoming involved romantically.

And what about her? She'd just had explosive sex with a man she had been lying to for years. A man from whom she'd withheld crucial information regarding the death of his wife. A man she would continue to lie to for the rest of their lives.

But there hadn't been any stopping either of them tonight. Their need had overwhelmed their common sense. They had come together as lovers, and couldn't seem to get enough of each other.

Now they had to deal with the fallout.

Ross came back in the room and sat down at the foot of the bed. They looked at one another for a minute. Her ardent lover was gone. In his place sat a man in abject misery. "I cheated on her," he said quietly. "I cheated on my wife." He took a breath. "I didn't mean to.

But I've been so lonely and you're so lovely. I wanted you and I took you. Now I feel like shit."

"Thanks," she said dryly.

"Wait. No. I didn't mean—"

Miranda held up her hand. "I get it. Believe me, I get it. Would it do any good to point out that your wife is gone? You can hardly cheat on a dead woman."

"I know that up here." He pointed to his head. "But not here." He pointed to his heart.

"I'm sorry, Ross. Being together tonight wasn't the best idea in the world for a lot of reasons, not only guilt. It probably shouldn't happen again."

"Which doesn't make me feel all that wonderful."

"Me either. But it is what it is. You're a recovering alcoholic less than a year into sobriety with a shit-ton of guilt to work through before you're going to be ready for anything. It's not the best idea for me either." *Because I'm holding onto a secret and I'm scared of what the truth about your cheating wife will do to you.* She lifted her chin. "But I'm not gonna feel bad about it. I'm gonna treasure the memory of this night. Of the whole evening, in fact. Thank you."

"You are most welcome."

She watched as he put on his clothes. He smiled as he leaned over and kissed her cheek. "I wish things were different, Miranda. I really do." She nodded. "I'll let myself out."

She watched him walk out of her bedroom. "I wish they were different, too, Ross," she whispered to herself.

She thought of the lies between them, and would always be between them. "More than you'll ever know."

Chapter Eleven

Ross

Miss Loraine pushed her shopping flat to the counter of the feed store and started unloading the contents. “You don’t have to unload,” Ross said as he stepped from behind the counter with the portable scanner. He turned over a thirty-pound sack of rabbit pellets and found the bar code and the machine beeped. “When did you start raising rabbits?”

Miss Loraine smiled. “It’s for my grandson’s rabbits. He’s gotten into them big time. Every time I turn around he’s having to build another hutch.”

“A hobby?” he asked as he unloaded a couple of big supplement bottles.

“Started out that way. But now he’s selling them, both pets and breeding pairs. He’s raising deer as well,” she added as he turned over a big sack of deer corn. “Selling breeding pairs to restock hunting ranches.”

“That’s interesting.” Privately he wondered why any rancher would need to restock deer, as plentiful as they’d become in the last few years, but he was no expert on running a hunting ranch. “Is he doing well?”

“He’s putting himself through college.” She beamed. “I’m so proud of him.”

Ross smiled. “You have every right to be.” His smile faded. So far he’d contributed nothing to the cost of his daughter’s education and that stung. Not that the Summersets couldn’t afford it. But Emma was his daughter and her education was his responsibility, not theirs.

Something else he needed to make amends for, and hopefully correct soon.

He rang up Miss Loraine's bill and loaded her purchases into her truck. Ray Martinez was waiting at the counter when he went back inside. He'd gone to high school with Ray and his late wife Tina, who'd died five years ago after a long bout with breast cancer, leaving Ray with three school-age children to raise by himself. The man had barely cracked a smile for years, but today his smile was wide and seemed to come easy. "I need you to show me something," Ray said without preamble.

"Sure. What can I show you?"

"The twelve-inch saddle on the back wall. I need to see if there are any options besides the one back there."

Ray motioned with his hand and Ross followed him across the big, dusty store to the saddle and tack section. His old friend pointed to a child's saddle slung across a sawhorse. "That one but more feminine."

Ross looked at Ray curiously. "We can get it in a couple of more feminine options. But your daughter's long past this saddle. Even if she wants a girly one, she needs an adult size."

"It's not for Becky. It's for Piper Zuniga. Heather's little one." He managed to look proud and sheepish at the same time.

Ross's mind raced. He remembered something, he wasn't sure what, about Heather's husband leaving her a couple of years ago. He lifted his eyebrow. "You and Heather?"

Ray nodded. "Me and Heather. We're getting married next month, doing a horseback wedding. Piper needs a child's saddle for the little mare she's riding in the wedding."

Ross smiled and stuck out his hand. "Congratulations, man. That's awesome."

"Thanks." They shook hands. "I feel like a new man. I still can't believe I've been so fortunate." His smile dimmed a bit. "After Tina died, I never thought I'd ever love another woman. I thought it was all over for me. And then I walked into Heather's classroom for a parent-teacher conference and *wham*. So here I am, forty-one years old with a whole new life to look forward to." He looked Ross in the eye. "I recommend it. Highly."

Ross nodded. He and Ray went through the catalog and Ray zeroed in on a saddle with pink and turquoise flowers tooled on the saddle and leather pieces. A phone call to the manufacturer and it would arrive this coming Friday. Ray left with Ross's sincerest congratulations.

Ray also left Ross with some serious food for thought as he took a quick look around the store to see what needed restocking. Love, and loss, and second chances for a whole new life crossed his mind, and not for the first time.

He'd been thinking about Miranda. She'd been on his mind for the last week, ever since he'd walked out her door in a fog of guilt and regret. He'd wanted her so badly that night, he'd ignored his own misgivings and the "wait a year" mantra preached by AA, and taken her into his arms. It hadn't been a booty call or a friends with benefits thing. What they had went way deeper. He wasn't sure what label to put on it, but it wasn't casual or meaningless. They'd connected on a level that cried out to be explored more fully. A level demanding a chance to grow into something deep and meaningful. A level that could grow into something permanent, if given the chance.

Which was why he felt so guilty. He wouldn't have thought twice about a booty call. That would have been only sex. But connecting on a deeper level had seemed like the height of disloyalty to the wife who'd always been loyal to him, even though he'd repaid her by becoming a falling down drunk.

He found himself staring at a shelf filled with insecticides, and got back to work.

As he barreled down the highway toward San Antonio and the theater, he thought about Renee and how she was gone. He'd loved her, he'd mourned her, he'd sat on her grave in the small cemetery on the edge of town and killed more than one bottle of Scotch while he cried until his whole body hurt.

He wondered if the time had come to move on. He would always love her. She'd given him twenty years of her life and a daughter he adored. Renee wasn't coming back, and Miranda was very much alive, warm, vital, and loving. She understood the battle he fought with his demons, having fought—and to a certain extent still fought—the same battle herself.

Once she'd become convinced he'd given up the booze for real, she'd been staunchly in his corner, sticking up for him at the theater and with the Summerset family. She was a good friend and mentor to his daughter. She was a good human being in every way possible.

Never mind the sex was unbelievably phenomenal.

In an odd way, he even had Renee's blessing. He remembered what she'd said on her way home from Tina Martinez's funeral. "I hope he moves on and finds love again," she'd mused. "He's too young for it to be all over."

"Would you feel that way if it was me?" he'd asked.

"Hell, yes. The last thing I'd want is for you to be alone for the rest of your life."

Maybe it was time to move on and see if anything could come of the connection he and Miranda shared. Hell, it was a lot to consider, but he hated being lonely, and she was so easy to be with.

He parked his car a couple of spaces down from Miranda's Beetle. He threw back his shoulders and stiffened his back, girding himself to get through another evening at the theater he still resented, despite the weeks he'd spent volunteering here. As hard as he tried, he couldn't warm up to the place. If only they'd called off rehearsals and sent everyone home before the storm had gotten so terrible. But they hadn't, and Renee had died on her way home.

It didn't get much simpler than that.

It was early enough to cut through the back. Josh snagged him as he came into the lobby. "Need you to sort and paperclip the ticket orders before you start with the t-shirt sales." He looked Ross up and down. "Trying out for a role in Oklahoma?"

Ross looked down at his tooled boots and western shirt. "This is how I normally dress. I had to come straight from work. Am I breaking the dress code too badly?"

Josh laughed. "It's no big deal. One of our favorite actors lives in snap-front shirts and fancy boots. I don't think Wade owns anything else." He handed Ross the ticket box. "Go for it, pardner."

Ross laughed and started in on the tickets. He had almost finished when Rachel poked her head into the tiny cubicle. "Okay, I doubled the tee and ornament order yet again. Betcha we don't sell out by the end of the Sunday matinee."

Ross grinned. "Betcha we do. Five bucks?"

"You're on." Rachel grinned and disappeared.

Ross finished the tickets and handed them over to the young volunteer who was manning the ticket line this evening. He didn't know what to make of it. Rachel and Josh had been downright friendly. They seemed to be warming up to him some. Unlike his sour-face former brother-in-law who shot him a go-to-hell look as he walked by.

He doubted Kevin would ever give an inch.

Not that he gave a damn, except for Kevin's possible influence on Emma.

Sales in the t-shirt booth were brisk as usual. The curtain went up and Ross occupied himself with freshening up the restrooms. He wandered over to where Kevin was unloading a case of beer into the ice cooler. "Need any help?" he asked, more to needle Kevin than for any other reason.

Kevin gestured to a box of candy. "Knock yourself out."

Ross pulled open the box and started unloading the candy bars. He filled the first bin and stored the rest under the counter and was unloading packages of chocolate-covered peanuts when Kevin said, "You're never gonna make amends this way."

"What way?" Ross asked with a calm he wasn't feeling.

"Volunteering here. At a theater you still resent the hell out of."

"I see. And why would you think I resent the hell out of it?" *Which I do, but that's not his business.*

"Your back's as rigid as a two by four and you have a sour pickle expression on your face when you think nobody's looking. You'd be a shitty actor, you know."

"Probably." He paused a minute. "You've got a wife now, right?"

Kevin looked at him. "You know I do. Letti and I don't exactly hide our marriage." He held up his left hand. A wide gold band graced his ring finger.

"And you and Letti have a little girl, if my memory serves me. Emily? Avery?"

"Everly," Kevin said tersely.

"The light of your life, I'm guessing." Kevin nodded. "Well, let me see if you maybe can understand." He held up his ringless left hand. "I don't wear my wedding ring anymore. No reason to. My wife's dead. She died coming home from here in a blinding rainstorm because a rehearsal ran late. Whoever was in charge that night didn't have the sense to knock off early and send everybody home. I'm down the wife I loved and the light of my life is down her mother. So forgive me if I'm a little pissed." He held up his hand when Kevin started to speak. "I take full responsibility for the drinking, and the fact that she most likely got involved here because she didn't want to be at home. But keeping her late at a rehearsal? Not knocking off, knowing a bad one was coming? That's on the Durango."

"But it's ridiculous to blame the theater," Kevin objected.

"Oh, really? How would you feel if it had been your beautiful wife?"

Kevin's lips tightened. "You're forgetting something. Your wife was my sister. I lost someone as well that night. So did Mom, and Dad, and Emma. But we don't blame the theater for it."

"No, you blame me. Because that's a lot more fun, isn't it?"

Kevin gasped. "That's enough, you two," Miranda said sharply. "I thought you'd both been told to behave."

"I wasn't aware I was misbehaving," Ross said quietly.

Kevin shrugged. "His truth and mine don't jibe. But then I don't expect they would."

"The truth? Like either of you knows what that is. The truth is like an iceberg. Most of it's below the surface. Very little is out for the world to see. Now, if it's not my imagination, I hear the last song in Act I and you're both gonna be slammed in about five minutes."

Ross nodded and stepped out from behind the concession stand. He wasn't quite sure what Miranda meant. Icebergs? The truth was below the surface?

It looked straightforward and clear to him.

He puzzled over her enigmatic statement until the curtain went down and he was inundated with customers. He worked the booth extra hard, not that he needed Rachel's money, but it would be fun to win the bet.

He then did his usual routine of freshening the restroom. Kevin waved him off, so he disappeared into the cubby and tried to read the latest download on his iPhone. But his mind kept wandering to the lovely woman who'd once again intervened in his dealings with his in-laws. Not that she'd necessarily taken his side this evening, but she'd most likely spared him an altercation, which was about to get loud and noisy, and most likely would have gotten him thrown out of the theater. Her eyes had sparkled even though her voice and expression had been stern, almost like a schoolmarm.

Why in the hell it made his cock hard, he had no idea.

Or maybe he did, as the memory of her naked body in the candlelight rose to taunt him. Her atop him, riding him as she moaned in delight, her hair wild around her shoulders and down her back, her breasts bobbing as she moved up and down.

He started to swell at the thought of going back to her place, of making love to her in the soft candlelight, even though they'd said it wasn't happening again.

He was beginning to wonder if it was such a bad idea after all.

His friend Ray sure seemed happy. The man hadn't smiled in years. Now he couldn't stop smiling.

It was time to face the truth. Renee was gone. He'd vowed "' til death do us part" and death had parted them. There was a lovely lady right down the road who was very much alive and who was right for him in more ways than he could count. He... No they deserved to consider the possibilities. They both had been through the fire, and had come out on the other side. It was time for them to see if what was between them was something they could build on. Share. Enjoy.

He had no idea how it would all turn out, but he sure would like to give it a try and see what happened.

It wasn't what AA recommended. But he really didn't care.

Now if he could only get Miranda on board.

He heard the finale begin and took his place behind the counter. As always, he sneaked a look at his daughter as she came into the lobby to shake hands. As he had every night, he hoped she would at least come over and speak with him. But, as she had every night, she ignored him. But he was making his point, he told himself for the hundredth time since he'd started volunteering. She was bound to get the hint sooner or later.

Unless his resentment was as obvious to her as it was to her uncle.

The first of his customers wandered up. Mindful of the bet, he continued with his efforts to ramp up sales and was smiling like a fool when he went with Josh to count the money. "Wow, you really outdid yourself tonight," Josh crowed as Ross handed over the proceeds.

"Cheap bastard doesn't want to pay up," Rachel teased as she stuck her head in the door. "Hey, Ross, you wanna join us tonight at Thirties? Throw back a few? Oh, wait, I guess you don't." She broke off and blushed furiously.

Ross smiled. “You’re right, I don’t. But I’m honored to be invited.”

“Tell you what. Sometimes we go out to dinner after the Sunday matinees. We’ll be sure to include you the next time,” she said.

“Thanks. I’d like that.” Not that his daughter would, but he’d cross that bridge when he got to it.

Traffic was heavier than usual on the Interstate, and it wasn’t until he took the turnoff to the farm-to-market road leading to the ranch he had the highway to himself but for the occasional white-tail along the side staring in fascination at his headlights.

Now he was almost to Miranda’s place, he felt an attack of nerves coming on. Last week she’d been as adamant as he was about starting a relationship. Presumably she hadn’t had any reason to change her mind. Whatever her reasons for not getting involved with him were probably still valid. If he wanted to start something with her, it would be up to him to change her mind.

Which was okay. He could do that. He wasn’t a dynamite salesman for nothing.

He pulled off the highway into Miranda’s place. Her car was parked out front and lights were on downstairs. Good. He took a deep breath and stepped out of his car. Her front light went on and she opened the door as he crossed the porch. “Ross, what are you doing here?”

“This.” He took her in his arms and took her mouth in a hard kiss. She froze for a moment, then she melted and her arms came around him, holding him close to her as she opened her lips. He kissed her thoroughly before raising his head. “We need to talk.”

She moved aside to let him in. “I thought we already did,” she said.

“What I have to say is different from the last time.”

“Obviously.”

She gestured to the sofa and sat across from him. He looked her in the eye. “I was wrong last week about feeling guilty. I have nothing to feel guilty about.”

“Knowing that in your head and honestly feeling that way are two different things. You knew it in your head last week. But not in your heart. What’s changed?”

“Ray Martinez.”

“Ray? What does Ray have to do with anything?”

"He was in the store this afternoon ordering a saddle for Piper Zuniga. He and Heather are getting married and Piper needs a saddle for the ceremony."

He watched as Miranda connected the dots. "So Ray's marrying Heather in a horseback ceremony. Good for them. I was afraid he'd mourn Tina forever."

"He's moved on and recommends it highly." He stopped and took a breath. "I want to do the same. I want to move on like he has. I'm not asking for a lifetime commitment or anything heavy. But I'd like to see you again. Take you out to dinner, spend time with you, and really get to know you over and beyond your friendship with Renee and the theater. See if we'd be good together."

"Spend a few nights together, too, I gather."

"What do you think? The sex was phenomenal. At least I thought so. You didn't?"

She gave him a "You're an idiot" look. "Of course the sex was phenomenal."

"Hey, I admit it, I'm lonely. If it's not my imagination, you are too. Together we wouldn't be so lonely. That would be worth a lot, don't you think?"

"It would. Yes."

"So how 'bout it?"

She bit her lip. "I still have reservations."

He sighed. "I know. It hasn't been a year for me. I get it. But I'm not talking permanent commitment. For now, I want to take you out and spend time with you. Have a little more phenomenal sex. Am I supposed to wait a year to go out on a date?"

"I don't know. I never thought about it. The one-year business isn't written in stone. It's a guideline." She fell silent.

"Is that it? Or are there other problems I don't see?"

She glanced to one side. Ross's eyes narrowed. If he didn't know better, he would say she was hiding something, but he didn't know what it could possibly be. She had nothing to hide from him. She had no reason to be anything but honest.

Maybe she was having second thoughts about getting involved with him, given his track record. If she did he wouldn't blame her.

She straightened and looked him in the eye. "You know what? To hell with it. I spent most of the week thinking about you naked and how much I'd like to get you naked again. Have some more great sex. It was damn wonderful, wasn't it?"

He breathed a huge sigh of relief. She wasn't going to turn him down. "It was more than sex."

"It sure as hell was, which is what scares me a little."

"I get it, and I'm with you, but I'm not gonna let it stop me."

He stood and pulled her up from her chair. "Miranda, we're doing this."

Chapter Twelve

Miranda

Miranda reached out and took Ross's hand. She forced her misgivings to one side. Things had changed from Ross's perspective, not from hers. The lies still lay between them. But he didn't know that, and she didn't think telling him would do any good. It wouldn't bring Renee back, and it wouldn't change where they were now. And damn it, she wanted him. She wanted to explore what both felt but couldn't define. She wanted Ross in her bed and in her life.

She would worry about how she'd deal with the lies in the morning. Tonight she was going to take him to her bed and savor every damned minute of enjoying what having him inside her made her feel.

He started to swing her up into his arms, but she laughed and took a step back. "The last thing you need is to throw out your back carrying me up those stairs again. I can walk."

"Run up them, you mean." His grin was teasing as he started up the steps with her at a speedy clip. They ran down the hall and into her bedroom, skidding to a stop beside the bed. She turned on the bedside lamp and Ross sat down on the bed and pulled off his boots. "Jesus, I need to take a detour by your shower," he said as he yanked open the snaps on his shirt. "I spent the day loading feed sacks and had to go straight to the theater."

"Hmm." Miranda pretended to think. "I imagine we can manage that. Leave your clothes on the floor and I'll put 'em in the wash for you."

He disappeared into the bathroom. He was already in the shower when she retrieved his clothes and ran them downstairs to the washer, which, along with the dryer, was housed in her large farmhouse kitchen. The shower was still on when she got back upstairs. Hmm. Too good an opportunity to pass up. She shed her clothes and walked down the hall to the bathroom, pulling aside the recently added glass shower door and slipping in the stall. Ross turned around, looking more pleased than surprised. “I wondered if you were gonna take the hint.”

“My mama didn’t raise no fools.” She snaked her arms around Ross’s neck. “I’ve been thinking about doing this all week.”

They kissed, long and lingeringly as water poured all over them. Then Ross picked up her shampoo/body wash and squirted it into her hair. “I’ve wanted to get my hands in your beautiful mane since I saw it down,” he said as he lathered her wild curls, kissing her as he massaged the soap all the way down to the tips.

She started to say something about the gray, but Ross had paid her a high compliment and she wouldn’t insult him by arguing about it. She poured a little of the shampoo into her palm and ran it down his chest, slowly drifting down to the nest of hair surrounding his swollen cock. “Gotta get you clean all over,” she murmured when he sucked in his breath.

“There’s clean and there’s *clean,*” he gasped as her hands surrounded him, smoothing lather onto his cock and balls. “You know, that goes two ways.” He dribbled a little more soap onto his fingers and teased open her lower lips. “How’s that?”

“Mmm, but no deeper. Sometimes I react badly to soap down there.”

“Oops. Sorry.” He grabbed up a washcloth and soaked it thoroughly before carefully washing between her legs. “Now, am I okay with bare fingers?”

“More than okay...oh,” she gasped. “Ross...*yes.*” She moaned as his fingers zeroed in on her nub. He caressed it with expert fingers, bringing her to a fast crescendo. She threw her head back as a hard, powerful orgasm tore through her body. “Damn,” she managed to get out as she caught her breath, “that was good. Your turn.” She sank to her knees and took his thick cock in her mouth. He was hot and hard and ready for her, and it took almost no time at all with her fingers and her tongue working him before he exploded into her mouth. “And we haven’t even pulled back the covers,” she said as he helped her up.

"I want to be inside you." He leaned over and kissed her swollen lips. "You think we could manage it in here?"

She looked up at him and shook her head. "With an eight-inch height difference? I doubt it."

"It's a wonderful fantasy." He grinned.

"Whatcha wanta bet the reality will be that much better?"

"I know it will."

They made quick work of rinsing their bodies and hair. Thick white towels waited for them on the shelf. They dried swiftly and wrapped the towels around them as they made their way to the bedroom. "Sorry about the hike," she said. "I keep threatening to build an en suite bath but other things get in the way."

"Don't. It would ruin the character of the house. Besides, who cares about where the bathrooms are when we have a whole week to catch up on?"

"Good point." She threw back the covers and shucked her towel, baring her body to the light of the bedside lamp. He dropped his towel on the floor and rolled in on one side of the bed and she the other, meeting in the middle for a sheet-scorching kiss that left them both breathless.

The sex in the shower had taken the edge off and now they could come together slowly, savoring every touch, kiss, and caress. Ross remembered what she liked and what she loved, and he used his knowledge to the fullest. He kissed her all over, paying special attention to her breasts and the sensitive spot between her legs, drawing two more earth-shattering climaxes from her before he rolled on a condom and slid between her slick, wet folds, his warmth filling her completely.

They began moving together, their bodies completely in sync. Miranda felt herself rising, starting to spin out of control. She could feel Ross rising too, but he seemed determined to wait for her to take her pleasure before he took his. When her body bucked beneath him and she let out a shout as delicious tremors tore through her from her core to her fingertips. Ross arched above her with a groan, pumping into her as he found his pleasure. Their release seemed to go on forever before he left her body and collapsed alongside her. "Damn, that was even better than last time, and last time was something else."

Miranda scooted next to him and kissed his bare chest. "Maybe practice makes perfect."

"Give me a minute and we can practice some more. But first I need to ditch this condom."

He got up and a few moments later she heard the toilet flush. "Pesky but a necessity," he said as he crawled back in bed with her.

"Maybe we could think about ditching them. It's been forever for both of us and I'm on the pill."

"We probably could." His stomach growled and he grinned sheepishly. "Sorry about that."

Miranda sat up. "Damn, if you had to come straight from work, you didn't get any supper. You should have said something."

"I was more interested in you than I was food." He sat up beside her. "But you can now feel free to feed me."

She wrapped herself in a terry robe and fished out a pair of her brother's sweatpants for Ross to wear. She took a quick inventory of her refrigerator as he followed her down the stairs, relieved to find that she could fix a speedy meal with what she had on hand.

His clothes were clean and she tossed them into the dryer. He set the table while she made grilled cheese sandwiches and heated a can of tomato soup. Tommy's birthday cake was long gone, but there was plenty of ice cream left for them to share.

With their passion temporarily slaked, they took their time, laughing and talking and enjoying being together as they made a feast of their midnight meal. By the time they were finished Ross's clothes were dry. "Do I fold them or do you want to get dressed?" she asked softly.

"Do you want me to stay over?" he asked equally quietly.

"I'd like that."

"Then I guess we better fold them so I'll have something to wear in the morning."

He carried his clothes up the stairs and left them on her dresser. "Are we going to sleep or for round three?"

She looked at his cock already at half-mast. "Shit, Ross. Three times in one night. I never heard of a forty-two-year-old doing that."

He pulled her into bed on top of him. "Take it as a compliment."

She tilted her head down to his. "Believe me, I do."

Chapter Thirteen

Miranda

Miranda stood beside Tikia and watched as Tony and Maria sang their last song together. Man, the cast was in top form tonight. They always did a fantastic job, but once in a while the actors, for whatever reason, were on fire, putting on a performance to bring the house down. Tonight was one of those nights. The leads had been amazing, and the supporting cast members had done their jobs spectacularly. It'd been a pleasure to watch Amy and Emma bring their characters to life. Amy had developed so much as an actress that she could probably carry a lead part sometime soon. Emma wasn't far behind. She soon would be gracing the stage as a lead.

Ross would be so proud.

She wondered if Emma would be speaking to him by then, or if the girl would continue to give her father the cold shoulder.

The rift between those two was heartbreaking. She thought Emma would've come around at least a little in the last six weeks, but the girl was as bitter as she'd ever been. Miranda was beginning to wonder if the Summersets were discouraging a reconciliation. Her gut instinct told her no. At least she hoped not. She had always been a good judge of character, and she felt like the Summersets were dealing fairly with Emma and Ross.

Unlike her. She was now lying through her teeth to all of them. Emma, the Summersets, and Ross.

Tony died and Maria delivered her last lines. Miranda pushed aside her thoughts and watched the finale, calling for the curtain to fall and then rise again as the cast took their bows. She jotted down a couple more notes, not that there would be much to go over with the crew chief tonight, and moved into the lobby.

Ross was stationed behind the souvenir counter as usual. Whatever he wasn't accomplishing with his daughter, he had sold the hell out of their *West Side Story* souvenirs, turning the counter into a serious money-maker, and proving himself a real asset to the theater. It was a shame they would lose him at the end of this production. Unless something gave with Emma in the next two weeks, Miranda doubted he'd come back.

The actors trooped up the aisle, and as usual Emma took her place as far from Ross as she could get. Which was fine. The last thing Miranda wanted was for Emma to pick up on the vibe between her and Ross. They'd agreed to keep their relationship on the lowdown at the theater. Not that Josh or Rachel would care. They'd actually warmed up to Ross and appreciated his salesmanship. But gossip spread faster at the Durango than a case of poison ivy, and if Josh or Rachel knew about her and Ross, it would be a matter of hours before everyone else knew. Especially Emma. The gossips would make a beeline for her.

Miranda and Ross were unwilling to risk the potential fallout.

She was lying to Ross, and they were both lying to Emma. She'd gone back to bed with him gladly, and he'd spent two nights with her since. When he was with her she was able to push aside her concerns, but after he left in the mornings, her guilt came flooding back, along with the knowledge there was no way this was going to end well as long as she continued keeping secrets from him. Yet, she couldn't bring herself to tell him the truth.

Knowing his beloved Renee had cheated on him not once, but four times, could, and most likely would, undermine his sobriety and drive him right back to the booze. If Ross knew, inevitably Emma would find out, as would the Summersets.

Miranda held fast to protecting Emma at all costs.

Even the corrosive guilt was better than that precious child finding out the truth about her mother.

Since there was nothing she needed to address with the actors, she ducked backstage and spoke with the crew and chief for a few minutes. The tail end of the audience was drifting out when she returned to the lobby. The actors were greeting their last fans and Ross was making a final sale. Emma spotted Miranda and waved to her. Rather than have Emma come to her, Miranda hurried over to where Emma was signing the program of a starry-eyed tween. "No, none of us are professionals," she was explaining to the girl. "We do this for fun. Are you interested in acting?"

The child nodded and Emma launched into a sales pitch for the Academy. "You can get started at any time," she explained. "They'll teach you everything you need to know." She jotted down the Academy's email address and their phone number on the program. "Have your mom or dad get in touch with Jessica Howard. She's in charge of the Academy and can explain everything."

The little girl and her mother thanked Emma before moving to the next actor. "Nicely done," Miranda said as she gave Emma a hug.

"She seemed interested and so did her mother. She's about the right age. I wish I'd gotten started sooner."

"You weren't much older than her. What were you? Seventh grade? Eighth?"

"Eighth. Almost in high school."

Miranda thought back. It was after Renee had broken up with her third lover. That's when Miranda had thought getting Renee and Emma involved might keep Renee too busy for any more affairs.

Fat lot of good it had done.

"You have nothing to regret. You're outdoing yourself in a significant supporting role and will easily be appearing as a lead before too long."

"Thanks." The girl glanced over to her father, who, with Josh, was walking out with the money box. Her lip curled. "Is he ever gonna quit coming here?"

Miranda hesitated, choosing her words carefully. "He seems determined to prove to you he's a changed man."

"He may be. But that doesn't mean I want to have anything more to do with him. Babs said I didn't have to if I didn't want to."

Miranda raised her eyebrow. "Your grandmother's talking badly about him to you?"

"No. She wouldn't do that. But she's not pushing me in his direction, either. She said it was entirely up to me. It's my choice not to speak to him. Not hers."

Miranda breathed a sigh of relief. "I see. It's your doing."

"Completely and entirely."

"It's not what your mother would have wanted," Miranda reminded her gently. "Cutting him off the way you have. But you already know that." She squeezed Emma's arm. "You think about it."

Emma acknowledged her with a curt nod and turned to greet the last of their patrons.

Miranda swallowed back the sour taste in her mouth as she sat down in her tiny office and changed out the batteries in her headset. She'd had to edit every word she said to Emma this evening. If she spoke up too much for Ross, Emma would get suspicious. The loss of spontaneity with the daughter of her heart hurt Miranda, but she didn't have much choice if she wanted to keep her relationship with Ross a secret.

Being a liar sucked. Big time.

Ross was waiting when she pulled up in front of her house. They were in one another's arms before they were even to the front door. They kissed their way up the steps and across the porch and into the house, strewing their clothes through the living room and up the stairs until they collapsed on the bed ready for each other. Ross flipped onto his back and pulled her down on top of him, entering her with a swift thrust making her moan. They rode the storm together, coming to a swift, mutual climax that had them both gasping. "Damn, it keeps getting better," she murmured as she collapsed on his chest.

Ross put his arms around her and kissed her slowly and tenderly. "It really does."

She rolled to one side and snuggled up next to him. "Did you sell a lot of shirts?"

"Same old same old." He looked at her curiously. "What did Emma have to say to you tonight?"

"Nothing that'll make you feel good." She laid her head on his shoulder and threw her arm across his chest.

"She's not giving an inch, is she?"

"She's a tough little nut to crack. And before you ask, the Summersets aren't behind it. They've chosen to remain neutral."

"If you say so." He kissed her lips. "Got the fixins' for another one of your midnight feasts?"

She cooked omelets and toast and he promised her a real date after tomorrow night's show. After they ate, he retrieved a packed duffel from his truck and they made love again before falling asleep in one another's arms.

He was gone by the time she woke up the next morning. She took care of her usual morning chores, decided to let a couple of the calves nurse another week before hauling them to market, and was showered and dressed and to the AA meeting with a few minutes to spare. Ross came in at the stroke of two. The only chair left was directly across from her. He caught her eye with a look that scorched her panties. She held his gaze, knowing she was looking at him with the same longing and desire. Miss Lorraine looked at them with a satisfied smile and Larry's eyes narrowed.

So much for keeping their relationship a secret from the AA group.

They welcomed a new member from out of town and addressed a few concerns. The meeting adjourned a little early, and Miranda was about to duck out and head for the theater when Larry cornered her coming out of the restroom. "Have a minute?" he asked quietly.

"I do." She had a good idea what this was about. Not a discussion she looked forward to.

He gestured toward the door leading to a Sunday School classroom. He shut the door behind them. "Do I need to take a seat?" she asked dryly.

"I don't think we'll be that long." Larry perched on the side of the desk. "Are you and Ross involved with one another?"

"What makes you ask?"

Larry's face turned red. "I saw his truck leave your place this morning. Early enough I guessed he hadn't come over for breakfast."

Miranda thought a minute. She could lie, bluff her way through this, or she could tell Larry it was none of his business. But he'd done too much for her over the years to dismiss his concerns would be an insult. He was Ross's sponsor and had a right to know. Besides, she needed to be honest with someone about something. "If you're asking if he spent the night at my place, the answer is yes, he did. And before you remind me, I know AA recommends no involvements for the first year. Ross knows it too. We got involved anyway."

Larry winced. "Not the best idea in the world, at least for him. To involve himself in a serious relationship until he's more firmly grounded in his sobriety and who he is is dicey."

Miranda smiled crookedly. "It's hardly 'serious'." She made air quotes. "Larry, I'm lonely. Renee's dead and my brother's gone.

Once I leave the theater I have nobody to talk to except my cows until I go back to work or come to AA. He's even lonelier. Renee's dead and Emma won't give him the time of day, and he doesn't have a theater to escape to. We enjoy spending time together and there's been a time or two we didn't have to call you because we have one another. I'm not sure how that's damaging to either of us."

Larry's expression was troubled. "I hear you, I guess. I suppose I was lucky. I've never had to do lonely. Thank god for my wife. She stood beside me through all of it. Okay, then. But be careful, all right? For both your sakes. There's a reason the organization preaches waiting."

"We will. I promise."

She was deep in thought as she drove toward San Antonio. Larry was right. The organization's reasons for recommending a waiting period were valid. They were playing with fire, even more than Larry could imagine with her lies thrown into the mix. But she wanted Ross. It had been years since she wanted a man the way she wanted him, and he appeared to want her as much. Too badly to walk away from one another. That wasn't happening anytime soon.

Not if she had her way about it.

***

Miranda ducked out of the back door of the theater and hustled across the parking lot to where Ross waited for her in his truck. She was tired and her head hurt a little. Half the Sunday matinee seats had been filled by students from one of the high schools. While the kids had enjoyed the performance, the audience noise level had been higher than usual, although the performers didn't seem to notice or mind.

A hot September breeze blew from the south and the sun's late afternoon rays scorched her skin. Next week would be the last weekend of *West Side Story.* But *Beauty and the Beast* was well into rehearsals and would open the middle of October, and in the next couple of weeks they would cast their winter production, *The Addams Family* musical. Admittedly an odd choice for the holiday season, but still a lot of fun. She was always a bit sad when one production ended and the cast and crew and other volunteers for that show disbanded. But many of the actors and crew would be back for future productions.

She doubted if Ross would be back. He'd gotten nowhere with his hard-headed daughter, and his early optimism had faded into understandable discouragement. "I don't know why I even tried," he'd said yesterday in AA. "I hurt her too deeply for her to forgive me."

"You tried because you love her and you had to give it a shot," Miss Lorraine said.

"Sometimes amends aren't made overnight," Adam had chimed in. "Sometimes it takes years."

Neither of which made Ross feel any better.

She hopped into his truck and he took off. The parking lot was mostly empty but he still hurried away from the theater so they wouldn't be seen together. "So where would you like to go on this honest to goodness date?" he asked as he turned toward the expressway.

"As opposed to all the booty calls and midnight suppers at my place?" she teased.

"For which I apologize profusely. I should've been doing the other: dining you without wining you, not showing up for wild sex after the show."

"One of the drawbacks of working in the theater. The good news is once *West Side Story*'s over next week, I don't have a production for another month. We can go on real dates. Not wining me, huh? What would that be? Orange juicing me? Perriering me? Coking me?"

"I was thinking more along the lines of steaks and Mexican food, and Italian dinners. So what'll it be tonight? Any of those tempt? Maybe a romantic dinner on the Riverwalk?"

"Wouldn't say no to the Riverwalk."

"Google the restaurants while I head on down."

She found a Mexican place that'd been around forever and made a reservation. He parked a few blocks down from the restaurant and they descended to river level. The crowds weren't yet up to their pre-pandemic levels, which was fine with her. The ambiance was as romantic as ever, and as the sun dropped out of sight in the west and the lights winked to life, their reflection sparkled in the rippling water. Ross took her hand and they strolled down the sidewalk in no particular hurry. "Feels good, doesn't it? To be walking out in public again." Ross squeezed her hand.

"We don't appreciate the simple things until we don't have them any longer," she agreed.

They were seated immediately on the outdoor patio, where they could watch the people enjoying the evening. The menu stuck to Tex-Mex tried and true, and it wasn't long before plates heaping with enchiladas, tacos, and guacamole sat in front of them. Conversation was spare as they dove into their meals. Miranda was hungry, having missed lunch to put out feed for the cattle. Her plate was empty before Ross's. He grinned wickedly and pushed the remaining chips toward her. "Didn't like it a bit, did you?"

"Not one bit." She dunked a chip in the salsa bowl. "Damn, this stuff's good."

Ross loaded up a chip and popped it in his mouth. "The best."

They laughed and talked. The sky faded to black and what few stars were visible through the city lights slowly appeared. Ross dealt with the bill and they joined the tourists and locals, holding hands and meandering down the sidewalk, soaking in the romantic ambiance. They were trying to decide if they were hungry enough for ice cream cones when they rounded a sharp corner and ran smack into Maggie and her boyfriend Kirby. Maggie stopped in her tracks and her eyes widened. "Uh, hi, Miranda." She looked from Miranda to Ross.

Uh-oh. Miranda's mind raced. The last time Maggie had seen Ross was the morning he'd been thrown out of the theater. She didn't know if Maggie knew he was volunteering or that he'd sobered up. What she did know was their relationship was no longer a secret.

Well, hell.

Nothing to do but to brazen it out. "How are you two? I don't know if either of you has met Ross Ellis, Emma's father. Ross, this is Maggie Gutierrez and Kirby Martinez. Maggie's our developmental director and Kirby has sent several lovely grants our way."

If Ross recognized Maggie, he gave no sign. Maggie recovered quickly and they did the "nice to meet you" routine and a couple of minutes of small talk before moving on. Ross's face was grim as

Maggie and Kirby moved on down the sidewalk. "I gather we're outed," he said quietly.

"Oh, yeah. You don't remember Maggie?"

"Aw, hell. Was she there the morning I got thrown out?"

"She was. I could tell she recognized you before I even introduced you, and I'd lay bets by noon tomorrow everybody in the office will know you and I were holding hands on the Riverwalk."

"How long before Emma knows?"

"Another day. Two at the most."

"Son of a bitch. I guess we should have holed up in Pleasanton."

"*No.* We shouldn't have to hide. We haven't done one damned thing wrong."

"Emma's not going to see it that way."

No. Unfortunately, she wasn't.

Chapter Fourteen

Miranda

The gossip mill was operating more slowly than usual, so it was Thursday before Emma stormed into Miranda's office. "What were you doing down on the Riverwalk holding hands with my father?" Emma demanded.

Miranda looked up from the wig she was designing for *Beauty and the Beast.* "We had finished dinner and were enjoying the river." She forced herself to remain calm in the face of Emma's anger.

"That's not what I mean and you know it. You're dating him, aren't you?" the girl spat out.

"I'm seeing your father, yes. Nothing heavy. The occasional dinner out. Maybe a movie now and then when *West Side Story* finishes up."

"You're taking his side? Damn it, Miranda, I thought you understood. My father—the things he did—he's despicable. He's awful. He's *horrible*. He's—"

"A recovering alcoholic who did some despicable things while under the influence. He's the first one to admit it and I'm the first one to second it."

"You know and you're still on his side?"

"I'm not on anyone's side. However, I see some other things about your father. He's a recovering addict who's determined to stay off the sauce. He's a grieving widower who put the love of his life in the ground. He's a father who's trying desperately to reconnect with a daughter who admittedly has good reason to turn her back on him. So yes, I understand, Emma. I understand all too well."

Emma curled her lip. "He must not be grieving Mom all that much, if he took up with you."

Miranda ignored the jab to her heart. “Don’t kid yourself,” she said more sharply than she’d intended. “He still misses your mother and will every day for the rest of his life. Exactly the same as you do. He misses you too. Why else do you think he comes here for every performance so you can continue to ignore him? A lesser man would have given up weeks ago. For crying out loud, Emma. Give the man a little credit.”

Emma’s face hardened. “So you are taking his side even though you say you aren’t. Damn it, don’t you get it? He was drunk most nights by the time I was in middle school. He neglected me and my mother for years. He was an ass about me going to the Durango. And then his last stunt at the Academy—that was too damned much. He was an ass, a jerk, a *drunk*, while Mom busted her ass trying to make up for it. He was too big a shit for me to forget it. Instead of understanding, you’re suddenly his biggest fan. Gotta wonder, Miranda. Is he that damned good in bed?”

Miranda sucked in her breath. “That was beneath you, Emma.”

“That’s okay. Because taking up with my father was beneath you. But you did it anyway. Jesus, is there anybody left I can trust now that Mom’s gone?”

“Emma, wait—” But she turned on her heel and was gone.

Miranda sank into her chair and put her head in her hands. *Damn it to hell.* It had been every bit as bad as she’d expected. Maybe worse. Not only was Emma still crossways with her father, she no longer trusted Miranda.

***

Ross

Ross rolled into the Durango parking lot and pulled into a space a few down from Miranda’s Beetle. There were plenty of cars in the lot already, and normally he would hike around the building rather than cut through the back and chance a meeting with Emma. But this afternoon he was willing to take the chance. He didn’t much care if his daughter would be upset by his presence. Hell, he didn’t much care if the entire cast was upset. He’d about had enough of his hard-headed daughter, the Durango, the AA group, and their dumb-shit plan for making amends to his daughter at the theater. The whole thing had turned out to be a clusterfuck. He was no closer to making amends to Emma than he had been when he returned to Pleasanton. He'd wasted countless hours and blown a shit-ton of money on gas running back and forth to the theater, time and fuel he could have put to better use. Now his daughter was on the outs with Miranda. If he'd stayed away, hadn't gotten sucked into this bullshit attempt to reconnect with the child who'd written him off, Miranda would still have the love and regard of the daughter of her heart.

But that connection had been broken.

Thank you, Durango.

He cut through the back and reported for ticket-sorting duty in the lobby. Thank god this lunacy was coming to a close. This was the last performance of *West Side Story* and he sure as hell wasn't volunteering here again. He forced himself to be civil to Josh and Rachel, returned Kevin's glare with one of his own, and plastered on a smile for his customers. He managed a small but genuine smile for Miranda, not surprised at her lackluster response. She was hurting as badly as he was.

He reminded himself volunteering at the theater had been her idea in the first place and he should be angry with her, but he couldn't find it in himself to be mad at her. Not when he'd seen how badly she was taking the falling out with Emma. Miranda genuinely loved his daughter. Hard to argue with that.

The afternoon dragged on until finally the curtain went down for the last time. The bows and curtsies went on longer than usual, but finally the cast lined up in the lobby. Most of the women held bouquets and the smiles all around were wistful. Miranda had explained that after working so hard together for so long, some of the cast and crew felt a bit bittersweet after the last performance. Which seemed like a crock of shit.

Maybe because Renee had always felt that way.

He sold the three remaining t-shirts as the last of the audience drifted out. He shut the lockbox and was putting away the handful of Christmas tree ornaments when Kevin appeared carrying his lockbox. "Josh said to meet him in his office," the younger man snapped.

Ross graced his former brother-in-law with a withering look and followed him around to Josh's office where Josh was seated behind his desk. “Let’s get this counted and get out of here,” Josh said. “Bubbe’s having me, Cameron and the kids to dinner.”

“And you can hardly wait,” Kevin deadpanned.

“Bubbe’s Miss Ella has a way with food like you wouldn’t believe,” Josh said.

Despite Josh’s supposed desire to hurry, he and Kevin continued to banter back and forth. “Can we get this show on the road?” Ross finally asked tersely. “I’d like to go.”

“Hot date?” Rachel’s eyes danced as she stuck her head in the door.

He gritted his teeth. “Not really.”

If Rachel noticed his ill humor, she chose to ignore it. She joined the banter, which dragged things out even more. Normally Ross would have been happy to join in or at least listen, but his nerves were at the breaking point and he wanted to get finished and make his escape. He counted his money, again accurate to the penny, and put it in the bank bag. “Here.” He shoved the bag across the desk. “I’m done.”

Josh looked up from the other pile of money. “Thanks for the help. Any chance you’ll be back for the next show?”

Ross huffed. “Not on your life.”

Josh’s jovial smile faded a bit. “That’s too bad. We appreciate your efforts. I’m sorry Emma didn’t.”

“That’s putting it mildly,” Ross said.

“We’re a bit disappointed too,” Rachel said. “We’d hoped you’d see the value in what we do here at the theater. Were you able to understand even a little why we love it so much?”

“Not really,” Ross said. “It’s a little hard to see value in the theater that’s responsible for my wife’s death.”

Josh and Rachel looked at one another, their smiles fading. “What the hell does the theater have to do with your wife’s death?” Josh demanded.

“It’s nothing, Josh. No big deal.”

Ross turned around, startled. Miranda was standing in the door of the office, shaking her head with a deer in the headlights look on her face. Ross looked from her to Josh. “It’s nothing, Josh. Really. Ross, are you ready to go?” she asked.

Josh shook his head. “No, Miranda, it’s more than ‘nothing’. This is the second time Mr. Ellis has said in my presence this theater is responsible for his wife's death. This time he said it stone cold sober. He's made it plain he holds this theater and everyone here responsible for Renee's death and I'd like to know why."

Three years of resentment erupted. "You know damned well why," Ross snarled. He leaned over and smacked his hand on the desk. "You held a fucking rehearsal the night she died. You knew there was a tropical storm blowing in. You knew driving conditions were gonna suck. But you held a rehearsal anyway. You kept your cast late. You kept them here until it wasn't safe to drive. My wife had a wreck in that storm, trying to get home. So yes, I hold the theater and everyone involved with it responsible. Got it?"

Josh and Rachel looked at one another and then over at Miranda. "Ross, I don't know where your wife was that night or why she was driving home so late. But she wasn't here." Josh looked at him with confusion.

"What the hell do you mean, she wasn't here? You were in the middle of one of your big rehearsal weeks. You don't call those rehearsals off for any reason. She was here."

"No, she wasn't," Rachel said quietly. "For the first and only time ever, we called off a tech week rehearsal. We knew how bad the storm was going to be and didn't want our people out in it." She looked at him earnestly. "I called her myself that afternoon about five and told her not to come in. She knew not to come to San Antonio that night."

Ross's head spun. "You're lying. She was here. She had to be here." He looked around, frantically trying to understand. "*Where else would she have been?*"

"I'd like to know that myself," Kevin murmured. "We thought she was here."

Miranda made a strangled sound. "Drop it," she insisted. "All of you. Drop it." She looked at them with an expression bordering on frantic.

"Drop it. *Drop it?* I will be damned if I drop it. Miranda, answer me. Do you know where she was that night?" Ross demanded.

"You don't want to know. Please, Ross. You really don't want to know."

"You really think I don't want to know where *my wife* was before she died? Tell me." He heard himself roaring and didn't care. "*Now.*"

Miranda tipped up her chin. "She was at my place."

"Bullshit. You weren't home that night either. You were at an AA meeting that ran late. You said so that night. What the fuck, Miranda? *I want the truth."*

"She was at my place," Miranda said quietly. "In the bunkhouse. With Butch."

Ross blinked. "With Butch?" He pictured Miranda's handsome younger brother and a sick feeling started to roil in his gut.

"With Butch?" Kevin echoed. "What would she be doing with Butch?"

"What do you think she was doing with Butch?" Miranda's lips tightened.

"That's a lie," Kevin objected. "My sister wouldn't do something like that."

"Yes, she would," Miranda shook her head. "And he wasn't the first."

Yes, she would. And he wasn't the first. Ross stared at Miranda in horror as the truth slowly sank in. *His wife had cheated on him.* She had been cheating on him the night she died. His beloved Renee had slept with Butch Jenks. She'd broken her vows with more men than just Butch.

He looked at Miranda. She looked back at him with a mixture of defiance and guilt.

Holy shit. Miranda had known what was going on all along and lied about it. Covered it up. Protected Renee and the bastards she slept with. Let him go on blaming the Durango when the theater had nothing to do with it.

The thought made him sick to his stomach. Both women had betrayed him. Renee had cheated on him repeatedly. Miranda had covered her cheating and then lied to him for years.

He wasn't sure which woman's betrayal made him angrier.

He whirled on Miranda, not bothering to hide his fury. "You covered for her. You kept her secrets and let her go right on lying to me, didn't you? And then you lied to me yourself. You told me she was at the theater. You let me believe that. You let me blame the theater when it was your brother's fault. You protected her and the bastards she slept with."

"You're damned right I lied." Miranda advanced on him, defiance on her face and in her voice. "And I'd do it again in a heartbeat."

"*Why?*" he roared. "Why did you cover her cheating?"

"Because of Emma." She poked her finger in the middle of his chest. "I was protecting your daughter. That precious child of yours. She already had a scumbag drunk for a father. She didn't need a scumbag whore for a mother."

He heard Kevin's sharp intake of breath and ignored it. "That's a bunch of shit and you know it. You were protecting Butch and Renee. You didn't want me to come after your brother with a pistol."

"You? A pistol? You'd have been too drunk to aim the damn thing."

Ross leaned down into Miranda's face. "You are a lying bitch." He enunciated every word. "You are no better than she was. And you know what? Your lies cost me my daughter. If I'd known Renee wasn't here that night, I'd have never blamed the theater. I'd have never given Emma shit about wanting to come here. I ran her off because of your lies."

"No, you ran her off because you were a whiskey-soaked drunk."

He turned on his heel and stumbled out of the office. Damn Renee, and damn Miranda. He practically ran through the theater and across the parking lot. His fingers shook and it took him three tries to unlock his pickup. The two women in his life he'd let himself love, and they'd both let him down in the worst way possible.

His hands were still shaking when he turned off the Interstate to the farm to market road. Yes, he'd fallen in love with Miranda, he realized to his horror. He'd fallen for her sometime back if the truth were known. Not that it mattered. He didn't trust her as far as he could throw her and doubted he ever would. Without trust, his love was worth nothing. All his hopes and dreams for a future with her had flown out the window. As had his hopes for a reconciliation with Emma. His future unfurled in front of his eyes, lonely and bleak. Bile rose in his gut and the old familiar longing engulfed him, making his heart pound and his mouth dry.

He'd never wanted a drink so badly in his life.

Chapter Fifteen

Miranda

Miranda watched as Ross stormed out the door and down the hall. "Son of a *bitch,*" she said, more to herself than to anyone else in the room. "That's the last thing he needed this afternoon."

"You stand there and say all kinds of shit about my sister and you're worried about *him?*" Kevin stormed. "I can't believe you'd say those things about Renee. She wouldn't cheat. She wouldn't do something like that, no matter how crappy he behaved."

"Like hell she wouldn't. For god sakes, Kevin. Grow up and take off your rose-colored glasses," Miranda snapped. "Your sister cheated on her husband. Four different affairs in a ten-year period. I know because I covered for her during every one of them. She'd tell Ross she was coming up here to go shopping with me and then go meet her lover at a southside motel. She'd say she'd been at my place if he asked about a four-hour trip to the grocery store. Hell, why do you think I got her involved at the theater? I thought maybe if she was busy enough, she'd quit the damned cheating." She turned to Josh and Rachel. "Sorry for the shit show," she said as she sank into the chair Ross had vacated. "You two didn't need our drama this afternoon."

Rachel waved off Miranda's concern. "Kevin, are you okay?" Rachel asked as she put her hand on his shoulder.

"No, I'm not. How can I be after what she said about my sister? That's not the Renee I knew. That wasn't the Renee my mom and dad raised." He looked at Miranda angrily. "That wasn't the woman who raised Emma."

"Really?" Miranda looked at him with exasperation. "Why the hell do you think I lied through my teeth for years? It wasn't the

Renee I knew, either. The Renee who stood beside me when I was at my lowest."

"Why did you lie?" he demanded.

"I didn't want Emma to know. I didn't want your sweet, precious parents to know. And I didn't want Ross to find out, especially now, as hard as he's fighting to stay sober." She felt tears gather in her eyes. "I didn't want him to find out that the woman he idolized and put up on a pedestal didn't deserve to be there." She swiped at her tears angrily. "You think carrying her secrets for years was fun? You try it."

"No, thanks." A tic worked in his jaw. "He drank. He drove her to it."

"No, she decided to cheat all on her own," Miranda shot back. "Yes, Ross was a drunk and a shitty husband, but showing up for the first booty call? That's on Renee. She made the choice. She made the decision to turn to other men. You know, maybe it *is* time for a little honesty about your sister. Maybe it's time you and your family took her off the damned pedestal you've put her on and admit that she was as much at fault for her crappy marriage as her husband. You've blamed Ross for all of it for too damned long and that needs to stop. Because believe me, your sister bore her share of the blame."

Kevin gave her his famous glare. "What about Emma?"

Miranda took a breath. "She doesn't need to know."

Kevin uttered a sharp curse and heaved himself up out of the chair. "I'm outta here," he ground out as he stalked out the door.

Miranda watched him go and then turned back to Josh and Rachel. "I wonder if he'll tell them," she said softly.

"Tell who?" Josh asked.

"His parents. Emma."

"I have no idea," Rachel said.

Josh asked, "What do you suppose Ross will do now that he knows?"

"I don't know," Miranda admitted. "I don't know him well enough to hazard a guess."

"Really?" Rachel looked surprised. "I thought you two were an item."

"'Were' is the operative word," Miranda said. "Sleeping together and knowing how he'd react to what Renee did are two different things." She looked from Josh to Rachel. "Shit. I got distracted arguing with Kevin. Something this big could be more than Ross can handle. I need to get to his place and make sure he doesn't open a bottle."

They looked at her doubtfully. "Do you think that's wise?" Josh asked.

"He's pretty mad at you," Rachel said.

"I don't care how mad he is at me. He needs to stay sober. Wish me luck." She grabbed her purse out of her office and left the Durango.

The sun shone brightly in the western sky as she roared out of the parking lot and took the expressway ramp. The traffic was heavier than usual and she cursed the slowdown as she drove through downtown. Her mind raced. It would be an hour or more until she could get to Ross's place if he was even there. For all she knew, he could already be parked on a stool at his favorite watering hole. The thought of it scared her half to death. The man she loved could not, *could not* fall back in the bottle.

Yeah, she'd fallen in love with him.

Miranda cursed the tears gathering in her eyes. Damn it. Loving Ross was the last thing she needed, especially as angry as he was with her. In all the years she'd known him, she'd never seen him as angry as he was this afternoon.

He felt betrayed, and rightly so.

The hell of it was that if she had to make the same decision all over again, she'd lie to him. She would do anything to protect Emma. She would betray the man she loved to protect the young girl who didn't need to know the truth about her mother.

It was a helluva decision she'd made, and that decision had risen up and bitten her in the ass.

The traffic finally cleared at the edge of town and Miranda floored the Beetle. It seemed like the trip took forever, but it was probably no longer than usual. She sped past the entrance to her own place and instead turned into the Ellis property five miles down. She noticed the hay field nearest the highway was starting to grow the grass Ross had sown in last month. But her attention was drawn to the gunshots coming from behind the house. *God, he's trying to kill himself.* She blanched and hit a pothole so hard she bounced. But then she heard more shots and relaxed. If he was still shooting, he hadn't put the bullets into his head.

At least not yet.

She parked by the front door and ran around the house toward the boom of a pistol. Ross was standing on the back porch, aiming his 9-millimeter at a whiskey bottle sitting on a hay bale about a twenty-five yards from the house. With hands that were steady, he took aim and fired, blowing the bottle to smithereens. He marched across the field and picked up another bottle out of a stack. He plunked it on the bale and stalked back to the house.

He took aim and fired. Again, the bottle exploded.

If he saw her he gave no sign of knowing she was there. He shot two more bottles before he finally acknowledged her. "Here to beg my forgiveness?" he sneered.

"No." She forced herself to remain calm. "Here to make sure you don't open a bottle."

He held out the pistol in a hand that was rock steady. "Nope. Sober as a judge. So you can take your lying ass right back down the road."

"I'm gonna go as soon as I know you're not gonna drink. Do you need to call Larry?"

"No, I don't need to call Larry." He took aim and shot another whiskey bottle. "Gotta make sure I can aim the pistol."

Miranda shrugged. "You've always been a good shot when you're sober."

He set up another whiskey bottle. "Tell me. Who do I need to shoot? Who were the bastards my wife cheated with?"

"Nobody you know except for Butch."

"And you of course protected him. Your beloved brother and my precious wife. You lied to cover their cheating asses, which makes you no better than them."

"Probably not. But I did what I had to do to protect your daughter. Besides, I owed Renee. She was there for me when my boy died and she saved my life when the drinking got bad. If it weren't for her, I'd be dead. So yes, I was loyal. I covered for her. If it makes me no better than Renee, I can live with that." She tipped up her chin. "Look, I hated lying to you. I always did. But your daughter didn't need to know the truth about her mother. She already had to deal with your issues. She didn't need to know her mom was no better."

"Did it ever occur to you that maybe if I'd known the truth, I might not have been such a shit about the Durango? That maybe I wouldn't have run my daughter off?"

"Being a shit about the theater? That's on you. It was more important to protect Emma's memory of her mother."

"I'm supposed to believe that? You weren't protecting Emma. You were protecting Butch and Renee and you know it."

"Believe whatever makes you feel better."

"I'd feel *better* if my wife hadn't gotten her ass killed coming home from screwing her boyfriend. Tell me, did my precious wife ever rank her lovers in bed? Were they that much better in the sack than I was?"

"She never said. Their appeal seemed to be they were sober."

He whirled around to face her. "Fucking low blow, Miranda."

"Why? It's the truth. Look, I'll be the first one to admit that Renee was wrong to cheat on you. She wasn't looking for sex. She was looking for attention and affection, which she told me she wasn't getting any from you. You were more interested in the bottle."

"That's right. Blame me," he spat. "She's the one who decided to cheat."

"Yep, that's on her."

"Spoiled society girl." His lip curled. "Byron and Barbara Summerset's precious little princess was so used to them dancing attendance on her she couldn't handle not being the center of attention."

"All true, but you knew she was high maintenance and you married her anyway. Jesus, Ross, she was wrong to cheat. We agree on that. But what kind of husband *doesn't even notice?* She had four affairs. She left signs all over the place. Did it ever occur to you to wonder why she got all dolled up and then took four hours to buy seventy-five dollars' worth of groceries? Or why she kept going into San Antonio to go shopping and never came home with bags? Or all those supposed movie nights with girlfriends when she didn't have many girlfriends to hang with? Damn. If you hadn't been in a drunken fog all the time you could've figured it out."

"I didn't think I needed to figure anything out." Tears glittered in his eyes and he glared at her angrily. "I *trusted* her."

"You also neglected her," Miranda pointed out quietly. "Your bottle meant more to you than she did. If you hadn't been drunk all the time and neglected her so often, things might have been different." She took a deep breath and it hurt. Her heart hurt. "I'm sorry. I'm sorry she cheated. I'm sorry I lied, and I'm so sorry my lies hurt you."

"But you'd do it again in a heartbeat."

She closed her eyes and hung her head. "I would. To protect Emma."

"Fuck you. I'll never trust you again."

She looked up and saw all his emotions playing over his face. "I'm sure you won't." She shook her head. "I didn't come here to argue with you."

"Then why did you come?"

"To make sure you hadn't gone off the rails and picked up a bottle. I'm leaving now. I won't be back. Please promise me, please, please, please don't let this rob you of your sobriety. You've worked too hard to get sober and stay sober to have this set you back."

"What's it to you?" he snarled. "You don't give a shit about me or you wouldn't've lied to me for years."

Miranda bit her lip. He would hardly believe her if she told him she loved him. "You're Emma's father. That's what it is to me." The tears in her eyes blurred his face. "We could have had something beautiful. That's why I came."

Miranda left. She made it back to the car before the tears started running down her cheeks. She felt hopeless. He wouldn't ever trust her again and she didn't blame him. She'd made the call to lie and now she was paying for it. She'd lost the man she'd managed to fall in love with after years of being by herself.

Her hands were trembling as she approached her driveway. She hit the gas instead and headed the car down the highway toward Pleasanton. The grocery store. They had a decent selection of wine and she could get a couple of bottles…

Jesus, what was she thinking? She jerked the car around in a U-turn and headed back toward her place. No way in hell was she going to drink. Yes, she was heartbroken. She'd finally found love again and it had blown up in her face. But she would not, *would not* throw away eight years of sobriety because of it.

She'd lost Emma and she'd lost Ross. Her sobriety was all she had left and she wasn't losing that along with everything else.

She pulled into her driveway and bumped up to her house. She made a beeline for the refrigerator and with hands still trembling poured out an entire bottle of flavored water, her poor but safe substitute for wine. She flipped open her phone and hit a familiar number on speed dial and waited impatiently while the phone rang on the other end. "Larry, it's Miranda. No, I'm not okay. I'm closer to taking a drink than I've been in years. I need your help."

Chapter Sixteen

Miranda

Miranda sat about mid-orchestra in the Durango and watched as Amy Castillo sang Morticia Addams' "Just Around the Corner" from *The Addams Family* musical. Her rendition of the spooky tune was spot-on, and under other circumstances Miranda would have been delighted they had someone so talented up for the part. But today her enthusiasm was seriously lacking despite the talented actors auditioning for roles in the dark comedy. She reminded herself her presence wasn't necessary. She had no input as to who was awarded the roles. Today she didn't even care who played the parts. But going home held no appeal either. It hadn't for the last week. She'd spent long hours at the Durango, looking for things to do to fill the hours there rather than go home to the echoing silence and the temptation on the shelves at grocery stores.

Yeah, she was still tempted to say "to hell with it" and take a drink.

The temptation was easing up, thank god. Larry had met her at the café Sunday night. They'd stuffed their faces with chicken fried steak and Larry had listened patiently while she poured out her heart. He'd refrained from reminding her of the pitfalls he'd outlined, limiting his remarks to words of compassion and encouragement. Since then, she'd made it a point not to go anywhere near the liquor aisle on her forays to the grocery store.

She wondered how Ross was doing and if he was staying sober. He'd been sober when she left Sunday evening. Pissed off as all get-out, but sober. She hoped like hell his sobriety was sticking, but she didn't think he'd welcome a visit from her to see how he was doing.

She would be the last person he'd want to see under the circumstances.

Which hurt. She missed him. She missed Emma. She missed them both so damn much.

Amy finished her song to kudos all around and would probably get the part. Which would please both Castillo sisters to no end, as Rachel was directing the show.

Kevin was next up to audition. She thought he might be trying out for Gomez, but instead he sang one of Lucas Beineke's songs. It would be perfect casting. Blond and boy-next-door handsome, Kevin would be perfect as Wednesday's wholesome Midwestern boyfriend. Kevin's wife Letti was up after him, and to Miranda's astonishment sang one of Grandma Addams songs and knocked it out of the ballpark. Letti Aldrete, aging diva was willing to play a *grandmother.*

Miracles were still possible.

Or maybe it was love. Letti had seriously mellowed since her marriage to a much younger man, and after giving birth to his child. Maybe Kevin's love for her had worked the miracle. It was good to see Letti finally happy. It was good to see somebody happy.

Miranda sure as hell wasn't.

She looked around at the remaining actors. Nice people, but nobody she cared about seeing audition so she slipped out and walked over to the rehearsal room across from her office, where the cast of *Beauty and the Beast* was rehearsing "Be our Guest." Letti had finished her audition for *The Addams Family* and was back in her role directing the candlestick and the teapot. Miranda watched for a few minutes. *Beauty and the Beast* was coming together beautifully, as would *The Addams Family.* Her curiosity satisfied, she left them to their work.

A quick wave to Josh and Miguel Abonce, who were conferring about something in Josh's office, and she headed to her tiny office. She sat down at her desk and started sketching the wigs she was designing for Morticia and Wednesday Addams. The first sketch was crap, so she ripped it from the sketch book and tossed it in the trash. She was about to do the same to the second when Kevin knocked on her door. "May I come in?" He looked at her hesitantly.

"Depends. Are you gonna holler at me?" She was in no mood to put up with any more of Kevin's attitude.

"No. I'm gonna apologize for being an ass and hope you can forgive me. I was wrong to accuse you of lying. You of all people would know what my sister was up to."

"It's all right."

"No, it's not all right. I was way out of line and I'm sorry." He stepped in and closed the door behind him. "I had a hard time believing it at first." He turned a chair around and straddled it.

"And now?"

"Yeah, I believe it. You wouldn't lie. When I told Letti what'd gone down, she said she saw Renee once with some guy at the diner close to her mother's house. Young good-looking stud."

Miranda made a face. "My brother."

"Ouch. Sorry. Anyway, I'm really sorry I went off on you like that. I shouldn't have."

"Don't beat yourself up. Sometimes I still have trouble believing she carried on the way she did. You were right about one thing. It's wasn't the Renee I knew."

"It's not the sister I grew up with. I guess that's part of why we assumed it was all Ross's fault their marriage was so bad. None of us would've imagined her cheating. I'm still having trouble believing it, even with what you knew and Letti saw."

"I get why everybody assumed Ross was to blame. That's how it would have appeared from the outside looking in."

Kevin looked at her. "Was living with Ross that awful?"

Miranda cocked her head. "I'll let you answer that. What are your memories of her with Ross?"

Kevin shrugged. "He was nice enough when they were first married. I was a kid, so there might have been stuff I didn't pick up on, but he always talked to me like I mattered and would take me for a ride on the tractor when we'd go out to the ranch. When Emma was little he was good about bringing Renee and Emma to the lake. She loved the water and he would take her out on his shoulders."

"And later?"

"He changed. It was gradual at first. We'd go out to the ranch or they'd come into town and we could smell booze on his breath. Then he quit coming with Renee when she'd bring Emma to see Mom and Dad. Then Renee quit inviting us to come over to see them. She admitted to Mom Ross was drinking too much and she was embarrassed. That's when Dad and Mom started picking up the slack for Emma's activities. They'd drive down to see her school programs and things at church because Renee couldn't count on Ross being sober enough to go. When Renee died it all went to hell."

"Okay, let's backtrack to after he started drinking and before Renee died. Was he ever abusive to Renee or Emma? Yell at them, hit them, throw things at them?"

"No. Absolutely not. Most of the time he was a cheerful drunk, at least until Renee died. Afterwards, Emma said the only thing he ever got ugly about was her going to the Durango." He looked at Miranda. "He was never cruel or abusive that I could see. Neglectful, yeah. He spent a lot of time in a drunken fog. Does that jibe with what you saw?"

"Pretty much. He neglected her and she ran around on him."

Kevin winced. "It was both their faults. We judged him too harshly. We shouldn't have."

"You didn't know that truth, any of you. That's on me."

He looked at her curiously. "Why did you cover for her? Or were you covering for Butch?"

"Butch? You gotta be kidding. He's a big boy who knew what he was doing and did it anyway. No, I covered for Renee. I owed her, Kevin. The woman saved my life."

"She got you to rehab."

"It was more than getting me to rehab. She was there every step of the way the whole time Tommy was sick. My husband had taken off, and I was coping by myself with a dying child. She brought meals. She brought Emma to the hospital to see Tommy, and the two of them would bring him care packages." She felt tears well in her eyes. "She sat right there beside me for the last two days of his life and held my hand as he died." She swiped away the tears. "She put together his funeral and the reception afterwards. When I started drinking I think she was crestfallen. She was coping with two drunks, and at the time I was in a lot worse shape than he was."

Kevin whistled under his breath. "I did not know all this."

"No reason why you would. The thing is, she didn't give up on me. She tried to get me to quit drinking and I wouldn't. When I hit rock-bottom, she got on the phone with my insurance company and found a rehab facility that would cover me. She put me in the car and drove two and a half hours one way to get me there. When my stay was complete, she brought me home and took me to my first AA meeting. She kept tabs on me for months after that. She turned herself inside out to help me. I owed her even if I didn't agree with what she was doing."

Kevin looked puzzled. "Sounds like she pulled out all the stops to help you. Why didn't she do the same for Ross?"

"She tried. The difference is I knew I was at rock-bottom and needed her help. He didn't. He told her he didn't have a problem and could stop any time he chose to. Which was horseshit and she knew it. She gave up on him ever changing."

Miranda considered what she was about to say and decided Kevin deserved to hear it all. At this point, all the damage was done. "You know, after the first affair, I asked her why she didn't divorce him. She said she couldn't handle a lifetime of 'I told you so' from your parents. Apparently, they were disappointed Ross was the guy she chose to marry. She told me they insisted he wasn't refined enough and they weren't compatible." She shook her head. "I don't know if that's true, but what I do know is Renee never could handle not being adored. When Ross fell into the bottle, she went looking for someone else to give her the attention she wanted."

Kevin's brows went up and shrugged. "I was too young to know if that's true. It wouldn't've been the kind of conversation my parents would've had around me, especially if they were arguing with Renee. And I'm sure as hell not going to ask them now."

"It'd serve no purpose."

Kevin nodded. "So you covered for her because you think you owed her?"

"I did owe her, and I didn't want to see her marriage tank. Stupid of me, really. I kept thinking a miracle would happen: he'd quit drinking and she'd quit cheating." She ran her hand through her hair. "Then there was Emma to consider. That precious child did not and does not need to know about Renee. Although now she's bound to find out sooner or later." She sighed. "Was I wrong to cover for my best friend? I don't know. Probably."

"Maybe not. None of us knows what we'd do in a given situation until we're faced with it. I have no way of knowing what I'd do, and anybody who tells you they know what they'd do is lying through their teeth."

"Well, you're considerably nicer than Ross. He told me I was no better than Butch and Renee."

"Ouch. For what it's worth, I think he's wrong. You did what you felt you had to do. You had reasons for doing what you did. Even if everyone wouldn't agree with them."

"The wrong thing for the right reason. It doesn't matter why I did it. The truth is out, and he knows I lied. He'll never forgive me for it." She wiped the tears from her eyes. "I've lost them both."

"I'm so sorry. I know you were close to Emma."

"The daughter of my heart. She already feels betrayed because I took up with her father. She'll never forgive me when she finds out I lied about her mother."

He tilted his head and studied her. "How close had the two of you gotten? You seemed awfully concerned about him the afternoon we found out."

"Close. We could've built something wonderful, but it got shot to hell."

"I thought there might've been something going on between the two of you, even before Maggie spilled the beans."

"You did?"

Kevin smiled. "Let's just say that neither of you could act your way out of a paper bag." Miranda knew she was shit at hiding her feelings. "You think there's any way you might be able to put it back together? Give things a chance to settle down and then try again?"

"No. I've blown his trust. Finding out Renee cheated and I lied about it was the ultimate betrayal on both our parts. I can't see Ross forgiving either one of us."

"What about Emma?"

"She's not likely to forgive me, either. She's at a place in her life where she needs certainty. Black and white makes more sense to her. All this is shades of gray."

Kevin nodded.

"What are you gonna do? Have you said anything to your parents?"

"No, and now I'm faced with the same choice you were. Do I tell them? Do they need to know the truth?"

"That's entirely your call. You know them better than I do."

"What about Emma? You said it yourself. She's bound to find out sooner or later."

"I still don't want her to know. She loves her mother's memory so much. Do we have to sully it?"

"Damned if I know."

Well, didn't this all suck.

Chapter Seventeen

Ross

Ross hefted the last of the rabbit feed into Miss Loraine's truck. "So the bunny and deer business is going well?" he asked as he loaded on a sack of deer feed.

"Oh, yes." Miss Loraine beamed. "My grandson's made enough in the last two months to pay his spring tuition."

"Quite the entrepreneur," Ross said.

"And the field's wide open. Why, with that pasture of yours, you could run deer instead of cattle. Or alongside them."

"It's a thought. Problem is paying for all the deer-proof fencing."

"Maybe someday." She lowered her voice. "Will we see you Saturday?"

"Yes, ma'am. You sure will." No way would he miss it. As badly as he was floundering right now, the AA meetings were more important than ever.

She looked at him shrewdly. "We've certainly missed Miranda. I hope she's not so confident in her sobriety that she's not joining us any longer."

"I doubt it."

Miss Loraine waved as she drove away. Ross sighed as he walked back in the store. Miranda hadn't quit going to AA. She was attending the one in Pearsall, forty miles away. She'd texted him the Friday night after the blowup.

Am attending in Pearsall. You stay with Pleasanton group.

He felt like a heel about it. She shouldn't have had to give up her AA group because of their falling out. At the same time, he was relieved he didn't have to find another group or face her across the circle. He wanted to keep his distance and she probably did as well.

Even though he missed her like a son of a bitch.

The day dragged by one long hour at a time. Not that he was in any big hurry to go home. Now that he was no longer volunteering at the Durango or spending time with Miranda, the nights were every bit as long as the days, and a hell of a lot quieter. He was lonely, and as angry as he was with Miranda, he could still admit he missed her. She was so full of life, and was easy to be with. She understood, which made her betrayal sting that much more.

His footsteps echoed in the empty house he was spending too many hours holed up in, despite working until sundown every night getting his hay fields restored. He missed seeing his daughter. The glimpses he'd caught at the theater didn't seem like much at the time, but they fed his soul in a way he hadn't understood until he wasn't seeing her anymore and he was forced to rely on pictures and memories.

To his enormous surprise, he missed the theater. He'd come to enjoy the camaraderie shared by the theater people. Rachel's gentle teasing and Josh's witty quips. He missed the enthusiasm of the audience and the fun of seeing how many t-shirts he could sell. He wished to hell he hadn't gotten into it with Miranda in front of Josh and Rachel. He'd repaid their kindness with yet another outburst and doubted he'd be forgiven a second time, even if Miranda was willing to go to bat for him again.

Not that she was likely to do so. He'd been a shit to her.

He'd had good reason, but he'd still been a shit.

He pulled into his driveway and looked at his watch. He had almost three hours of sunlight left and another half hour after sundown before it got too dark to work. He changed out his work clothes into a pair of old jeans and long-sleeve t-shirt. He hiked out to where he'd left the tractor parked in the middle of the peanut field and started it up, plowing and fertilizing the loamy sand he would sow with peanuts come spring. He wondered if there was any point in continuing his efforts on his ranch. The way things were going in his life, he was sorely tempted to put the place on the market and go back to work on the ranch in Montana. They'd take him back in a heartbeat, and he would be gone from this lonely place. Gone from the memories, the daughter who refused to forgive him, and the women who'd broken his heart.

The October sun was warm on his shoulders, but not blisteringly hot like it had been a month ago. Mindlessly he drove the tractor up and down the field, the plow cutting furrows in the soil for the fertilizer to nourish.

With no real need to concentrate, his mind drifted back to the fateful afternoon at the Durango and the nasty, ugly truth he'd learned. Now that he'd had a month to think about it, he realized he shouldn't have been surprised about Renee. The signs had been there, even with Miranda providing cover. He should have wondered what Renee'd been up to. The numerous unexplained absences. The whispered phone calls out of earshot. The cheap gifts that seemed to thrill her so. The way she would jump in the shower and run her clothes through the wash the minute she walked in the door. An imbecile could have figured it out. He'd have caught on in a flash if he'd been paying attention, which would've required him being sober.

But that was the catch. He hadn't been paying attention. He was drunk almost all the time. He'd been neglecting her. Miranda had been right. The only thing he'd paid attention to the last years of his marriage was where his next bottle of booze was coming from. The loneliness had gotten to be too much for his needy wife, and she'd started having affairs. The affairs were on her.

The neglect and the drinking were on him.

The lies were on Miranda.

He swung the tractor around and started making another row. He had almost gotten his head around Renee's cheating. He had yet to come to terms with Miranda lying about it, even after they'd become lovers.

He wasn't sure why Miranda's duplicity hurt so much more than Renee's. But for whatever reason, it did. Maybe it was because Miranda's lying was so recent, and Renee had been dead over three years. Her sins were buried with her. Miranda's were still fresh. She'd lied to him from the beginning and continued to lie to him after he'd sobered up and deserved the truth.

She said it was to protect Emma.

Which was bullshit.

He had no intention whatsoever of telling Emma of Renee's adultery. He'd never want his daughter to know. The secret would have been safe with him.

But he'd deserved the truth.

He made another turn of the tractor. Thing was, he missed Miranda. Badly. Despite her dishonesty, he'd fallen for her like a ton of bricks. He still rolled over and reached for her in the morning, before he woke completely and remembered what happened.

The short month he spent as the man in her life had been everything he'd ever dreamed of in a relationship. More than once he'd picked up his phone to call or text, to reach out to her. But he hadn't done it. And he wouldn't. He was still too angry and too hurt by her dishonesty. He loved her, but he no longer trusted her. And love without trust wasn't worth shit.

He plowed two more rows. Five or six more and this field would be done. He was about to pat himself on the back for getting finished tonight when a car pulled into his drive and bounced its way toward the house. Somebody took the wrong turnoff, he thought. Probably looking for Miranda's place, or the Wilton's two ranches down.

He'd keep working and let the misdirected driver figure out on their own they weren't where they wanted to be. But whoever it was pulled up in front of the house and parked like they belonged there. He took another look at the expensive car. *Shit.* He hoped it wasn't who he thought it was.

His hopes were dashed when he recognized the full shock of white-blond hair as his former father-in-law stepped from the sedan. He groaned out loud when the passenger side opened and his perfectly coiffed former mother-in-law got out. She followed her husband up the steps and knocked on his front door.

Damn it to hell. What were they doing here?

He felt a moment of panic, afraid something bad had happened to Emma, before common sense took over. If something had happened to his daughter, someone would have called or texted him. Most likely Miranda. The Summersets wouldn't have driven over an hour one way to deliver the news in person.

Which meant they wanted to have a talk with him. *Shit. Shit. Shit.* The last thing he wanted tonight was to deal with the Summersets. It was tempting, so tempting to pretend he didn't see them and hope they took the hint and left. But they had done too much for Emma for him be a coward. Besides, if they'd driven all the way out here, they had something to say they thought was important. He'd let them say it, whatever shit they wanted to heap on his head, and then they would be on their way.

So much for getting the field plowed.

He killed the engine and strode across the field, willing away the anxiety. His last two exchanges with Byron Summerset had been rancorous in the extreme and he didn't look forward to another. Not that it would matter. He climbed the steps to the front porch and nodded to the two of them, who were sitting in the porch swing with solemn faces. "Byron. Barbara. What can I do for you this evening?"

They rose and looked at one another uncertainly. "We'd like to talk to you," Byron said quietly.

"If,,,if it's okay," Barbara stuttered. His former mother-in-law had struggled with a stutter her entire life. The more ill at ease she was, the more pronounced the stutter.

From the way she struggled to get that simple sentence out, she must be damned uncomfortable tonight.

He ushered them into the living room. "Have a seat. Can I get you anything to drink?" he offered.

Byron ran his hand down the side of his face. "I could use a stiff whiskey, but I guess that's no longer offered in this house."

Well, that was taking the bull by the horns. "No whiskey in the cabinet these days. I can offer you some ridiculously expensive coffee if you'd like. Or bottled water or a soda."

"Some of that fancy coffee would be nice," Byron said.

"Y-yes, it would," Barbara added.

His mind raced while the coffee brewed, wondering what had been so all-fired important. The Summersets both took their coffee black, so he poured them each a cup and delivered it to them before retrieving one for himself. He slid down in the chair across from where they were seated together on the sofa. "What can I do for you this evening?" he asked them for a second time.

"Kevin told us," Byron said without preamble. "About Renee."

"*Damn,*" Ross breathed. "I wish to hell he hadn't." He looked at them. "I'm sorry you found out." *Oh no.* He hoped... "He didn't tell Emma, did he?"

"N-no, j-just us," Barbara said.

"He took us out to dinner so he could be sure she didn't overhear anything," Byron assured him.

Ross breathed a sigh of relief. "I don't want her to know," he said firmly. "She puts Renee up on such a pedestal. I don't want her to know that...that—" he broke off and gestured helplessly.

"That her mother broke her marriage vows," Byron said diplomatically.

Ross nodded. "Yeah. That. She needs to remember her mother in the best light possible. Especially since she knows I've been no prize."

"Y-you d-didn't know?" Barbara asked. "A-about Renee?"

"No, I didn't. Not until Miranda was forced to tell me. I never suspected a thing." He ran his hand across the back of his neck. "I didn't pick up on the signs. They were there but I ignored 'em."

"So did we," Byron admitted. Ross's head snapped up and he stared at his former father-in-law. That was the last thing he expected the man to say.

"No reason for you to pick up on them. I didn't."

"Y-yes, but w-we were s-s-sober," Barbara said solemnly.

Nothing like sticking in the knife. "I suppose you have a point," he replied coolly.

"Maybe none of us wanted to see the signs," Byron suggested. "And then she died and we really didn't want to own up to anything. At least Barbara and I didn't. We weren't about to admit our daughter was less than perfect."

"And I went on blaming the theater because that's what I'd been led to believe. And ran my daughter off because of it," Ross said bitterly.

"I-It was m-more than t-the th-theater," Barbara said.

"Yes, I know," Ross snapped. "I was a drunk. I get that. I lost Emma because of it." He stopped and took a breath. "I lost both of them because of it. Finding out about Renee at this late date really doesn't make a lot of difference. She's just as dead, and Emma's just as gone. The only difference is that I'm lonely and sober. Not lonely and drunk."

"Actually, that's what we came out here to talk to you about. Emma," Byron said.

"What about Emma? Do you need help paying her tuition? Do I need to write you a check?"

"Nothing like that," Byron said quickly. He took a deep breath. "After talking with Kevin, we had a long talk with Miranda. We had questions for her."

"We all did," Ross murmured.

"She answered our questions honestly, even when they didn't put her in the best light. While Barbara and I don't condone her dishonesty about the night Renee died, she was trying to protect our granddaughter and our daughter. Hard to argue with that."

Not really.

"She also told us flat-out about all the covering she did for our daughter over the years. Frankly, we were stunned."

"So was I," Ross said.

"At first we didn't want to acknowledge it. But she convinced us. Said Renee was as much to blame for wrecking your marriage as you were. Forced us to see the truth."

"For whatever good it'll do," Ross murmured.

"She also weighed in on Emma. Said our granddaughter needs her father, whether she thinks she does or not," Byron said.

"S-she said-d Emma m-isses you. E-even if she d-doesn't w-want to adm-mit it," Barbara added.

Byron looked Ross in the eye. "She also said we need to use our influence to help you and Emma find your way back to one another. She was most insistent."

"I see."

"B-but b-before we d-do, that, are y-you g-gonna stay s-sober?" Barbara asked.

Ross tightened his lips. "What kind of question is that?"

"A fair one," Byron said. "I've got to be honest. We're not here to apologize for criticizing you in the past. You drank too much. You're a good part of what went wrong in your home. But our daughter was at fault too. Renee was in the wrong and it got her killed. Emma's lost her mother, but she still has her father. If you're sober for real, if you're committed to changing your life, we want to do what we can to see some kind of reconciliation between the two of you."

Ross dug into his pocket and handed his chip to Byron who fingered the medallion. "What's this?"

"An AA chip. Eleven months. I'll get my one-year chip next week. It means I haven't had a drink in a year," he said patiently when Byron continued to puzzle over the chip. "It means I've been going to AA. It means I'm committed to staying sober."

"Okay, then." Byron handed the chip back. "We'll do what we can."

"I appreciate it, but don't get your hopes up," he said. "Emma hates me. I don't know how much she told you about the ugly confrontation at the Durango, but she slapped the fire out of me and told me she hated me. I have no doubt she still does. I volunteered at the theater for six weeks trying to make amends and didn't get so much as a glance from her."

"You m-may be r-right," Barbara said.

"But then again you might not be. I'll plead your case." Byron puffed out his chest a bit. "I'm not one of the best courtroom litigators in San Antonio for nothing."

"I appreciate it."

But it wasn't going to do much good, he thought as he stood on the front porch and watched the Summersets drive away in the evening gloom. Not that he didn't appreciate what they were trying to do for him. They'd gone out of their way to come out here and talk, and he had no doubt Byron would do his best to plead Ross's case. Barbara would do what she could. But Ross knew his daughter. He'd shit in his Post Toasties with her and she'd made up her mind.

Emma wasn't up for a reconciliation and never would be.

Chapter Eighteen

Miranda

Miranda sat in the back of the auditorium and watched the actors working on the dances in the second act of *Beauty and the Beast.* Although tech week didn't start until the following Sunday, the actors were going over their dance steps on the stage. Jessica and Letti sat in the front row, each with a sleeping toddler in a stroller beside them. The actor playing the beast was a good if not great dancer, but the girl playing Belle had two left feet and had almost lost the role because of it.

"No, Tammy, it's step-step-glide," Jessica said patiently as Letti chewed the end of a pencil. "Justin, it's a waltz and you're supposed to be leading, so lead." She signaled the girl at the sound board. "Please take the dance number from the top."

Miranda shook her head as Justin valiantly led Tammy through the simple dance steps before the singing started. Tammy's voice was amazing, making up at least some for her serious lack of grace. Miranda reminded herself it was a week and a half before opening night and a lot of improvement would come to pass between now and then.

She hoped.

She watched for a few more minutes. Everly woke and immediately set up a howl to get out of the stroller. Letti looked around frantically before starting up the aisle with the unhappy child. Miranda rose and met them at the end of the aisle. "Want me to take her?" she asked.

"Would you? Mostly she wants out of the stroller, but there's new diapers and a bottle of orange juice under the seat. If the juice doesn't work there's animal crackers in a plastic bag."

"Or I could just let her loose." Miranda laughed out loud at the look on Letti's face. "I know better than that, Mom. We'll be in my office. Take your time."

"Thanks, Aunt Miranda."

Letti started back down the aisle. "I remember that howl," she said as she wheeled Everly toward the offices. She unlocked her office and lifted out the protesting child. "Yep. Soaking wet." She laid Everly on her desk. "No worries, little one. We'll get you fixed up."

Miranda stripped off the wet diaper. Everly quieted down and stared up at Miranda with puzzlement. "Don't know me, do you, Everly?" she asked as she spread out a clean diaper and quickly fastened it on the small-boned girl. "You know, you look more like your mommy than your daddy, but those pretty eyes are pure Summerset." She scrounged around in the bottom of the stroller and found the bottle of juice. Everly's eyes lit up and she reached for the bottle. "Here you go, sweetie." She propped the baby on her lap and handed her the juice.

The baby latched onto the bottle and sucked greedily. Miranda's mind wandered back to when Tommy and Emma were this age. Her memories were mostly of feeding Tommy, but she'd given Emma plenty of bottles as well while the young wives bonded over chasing a couple of active toddlers.

She was deep in a memory when staccato footsteps marched down the hallway. "Damn it, Josh, we don't need to hire that man," Rachel snapped. "There are plenty of other carpenters we could find who'd do every bit as good a job as he would."

"No, there aren't." Josh sounded annoyed. "We're not looking for a carpenter, we're looking for a set designer."

"Set designer, carpenter, whatever. We can find another set designer who's as good as he is."

"No, we won't. Cameron and I went over to the senior center and checked out his work. He's excellent. Phenomenal. We won't find anybody any better than he is."

"I don't care. We don't need somebody like *him* in the theater. Not with his past."

"His past won't make a bit of difference when it comes to doing his job. Besides, he's an old friend of Miguel's. Miguel Abonce. Our benefactor, Miguel. The one who rents this place to us for a dollar a year. The one who's called in a favor and asked us to hire him. So we're going to hire him."

"But...but—"

"Quit wasting your breath. The decision's been made."

"It's going to bite you in the butt when the Academy parents find out." Rachel's office door slammed shut and a moment later Josh's did also.

What the hell was that all about?

Miranda shrugged. Not her problem. The baby made short work of the bottle and chattered at Miranda for a few minutes before her little eyes grew heavy and finally drifted shut. She snuggled the sleeping baby close. She wasn't interested in raising another child, no way in hell, but it was nice to hold someone else's for a few minutes, feel a warm soft little one in her arms and smell the aroma of clean, sweet kid.

She had just laid Everly in the stroller when Emma poked her head in the door. Miranda tensed. It had been six weeks since Emma had found out about her and Ross and over a month since the blow-up with Ross and Kevin. There had been plenty of time for Emma to find out about her mother, although Miranda still hoped it wasn't the case. She looked at Emma warily. Emma looked back at her every bit as uncertainly. "Letti sent me to get Everly. Kevin's taking an evening exam and can't come get her."

"She's dry and just had a fresh bottle. Do you have a car seat?"

She held up a set of keys. "I'll drive Letti's car." She looked around. "Can we talk?"

Miranda looked at her with surprise. That was the last thing she would've expected from Emma. "You want to talk to me?"

"I have questions only you have the answer to. Do you have a few minutes?"

Uh-oh. *She knows.*

And if she knew, she had questions.

"Guess so. Come in and have a seat."

Emma pushed the door shut behind her and sat down across from Miranda. She drummed her fingers on the desk, a surefire indication she was nervous. "They told me. Pops and Babs. They told me the truth about Mom."

"Damn it," Miranda ground out. "I didn't want you to know. Hell, I didn't want them to know. I gather Kevin told them. I'd hoped he wouldn't."

"You didn't want anybody to know."

"No, I didn't. I'd hoped even if your grandparents found out, they wouldn't tell you."

"I don't think they wanted to. The only reason they did was because they want me to go out and see my father and I flat out refused. Babs said I needed to understand my father wasn't the only one at fault for what went down."

"He wasn't. Your mother bore her share of the blame."

"So why hide it? Why lie to everyone about it for years?"

Miranda sighed. "The truth? I was mostly trying to protect you."

"The whole time? Miranda, come on. If Babs and Pop got the story right, you covered my mother's ass for years while she carried on and continued to lie about it after she died. You even said she was at the theater the night she died when she was at your place with your brother. You expect me to believe you did all that for me?"

"Mostly, yes. Sure, I was covering for your mother and trying to protect your grandparents from the truth. Later I was protecting a fragile recovering alcoholic I was afraid the truth would drive back to drinking. But mostly I was protecting you."

"Why? I didn't need protecting."

"You didn't?" Miranda asked softly. "Emma, you were only ten when the affairs started. You were little girl whose daddy was drinking too much, and you loved your mother, and you looked up to her. You didn't need to know she had feet of clay."

"Why'd she do it? Why'd she start cheating on my father?"

"Her life sucked. Her husband and her best friend were both falling in the bottle. She was trying to cope with two drunks and raise you. Then along came a smooth-talking charmer who made her feel special, who paid her the attention she wasn't getting at home. I didn't know at first, didn't find out until I got out of rehab and realized she was using me to cover for the hours she spent with him."

Emma winced. "I had no idea. I never suspected a thing."

"Why would you? You were a kid."

"Okay. You covered for her and lied for her because you wanted to protect me. Didn't that bother you?"

"Hell, yes it bothered me." Miranda didn't try to hide her indignation. "It bothered the crap out of me. But the thought of you knowing the truth, of you knowing what your mother was doing, bothered me a whole lot more. You needed one parent you could look up to and it sure as hell wasn't gonna be your father. At least not at that point. Did I do the right thing? I believed so at the time. Still do, even though it's blown up in my face royally."

"So why didn't you tell Daddy what was going on? Maybe he could've stopped it. Or couldn't you at least have threatened her with the truth? Maybe she would've stopped."

"It was the plane tickets."

"What plane tickets?"

"Your mother had two plane tickets. One-way to Chicago. Her first lover had moved there and wanted her to come to Chicago and bring you with her. She was on the fence. She didn't know if she wanted to go. When I threatened to go to Ross about the affair, she said if I did she'd be on the plane so fast my head would swim." Emma gasped. "She would've done it. She would've moved you away from your father and grandparents. She was an inch from going anyway.

"I figured covering for her was better than having her leave. She broke up with him a few months later and replaced him with the next one, but it was always in the back of my mind that she was perfectly capable of taking you and running and I didn't want that. I loved you too much, and I knew ripping you away from your father and your grandparents for her selfish needs was a terrible thing to do. I guess if it boiled down to lying for her or letting her take you away, I'd tell the lies. I never gave up hope your parents would find a miracle and he'd quit drinking and she'd quit cheating."

"Which didn't happen."

"Part of it did. Your father's sober now."

"Does Daddy know?"

"About your mother? Yes. But he didn't know until about a month ago. Josh wanted to know why your father kept blaming the Durango for her death, and that's when he learned there were no rehearsals the night your mother died. He doesn't know about the plane tickets or how close he came to losing you both."

"Well now he won't blame the theater for everything," Emma said.

“Yep. Now he blames me. It’s all my fault for lying about the theater and his getting crossways with you.”

“There was a whole lot more involved in getting crossways with me and he knows it,” Emma stated.

“Yes, he does, and regrets the hell out of all of it.” Miranda took a deep breath. “Look, be mad at me if you must. I’m not asking you to forgive me. I lied through my teeth to everyone for years. But please, *please* find it in your heart to forgive him. He’s done some heavy lifting this year and he’s done it by himself.

“He beat Covid, he kicked a fifteen-year drinking habit and he’s trying to restore his ranch and rebuild his life all by himself. He’s turned his life around. But it’s hard going. Having been there and done that, I promise you it’s no easy thing and he desperately needs your support. He loves you and he needs you. He tried to make amends and if you give him a chance he’d make amends every day for the rest of his life.”

“What about you? What about your support?”

“I’d be glad to offer him that support if he wanted it. But he doesn’t. He found out your mother and I lied to him and his sense of betrayal is too deep.” She felt her eyes fill with tears and cursed inwardly when one ran down her cheek.

Emma stared at Miranda. “You really care about him, don’t you?”

“I do. He’s a good man. I’ve known him since we were kids. He’s back to being the person he was for most of his life. He deserves to have his daughter forgive him for being human. He’s your dad, and he loves and needs you.” She sighed. “It’s okay if you don’t forgive me. I know I’ve lost you. But don’t lose your dad.”

“You haven’t lost me. I’m pissed off at you for lying, but it’s kinda hard to stay pissed off when I know you lied because you were trying to protect me. You’re the closest thing I have to a mother, and mothers and daughters have their moments. We’re okay, Miranda. For real.”

“Thank you, honey.” Miranda stood, opened her arms and gathered Emma close. They held on to one another for a long time, shedding a few tears together. When they moved apart, Miranda stepped back. “I want you to listen to me. Forgive your father.”

“I’m not sure I can.”

"It's important, Emma. Please, reach down in yourself and find a way to forgive him. I know he was absent when you needed him, and he hurt you. But he was a good husband and father before the drinking took hold of him, and he's worked hard to change. He needs you, and you need him."

Emma nodded. "I'll think about it." She brushed a kiss across Miranda's cheek. "We'll get together for lunch sometime soon." She turned to the baby. "Come on, little one. Aunt Emma needs to get you home."

Miranda's eyes swam with tears as Emma shut the door behind her. Tears of gratitude that she and the daughter of her heart had found their way back to one another. But that was only half the battle. Emma needed her father. *Please let her and Ross find their way to one another again. They need each other so much.*

Chapter Nineteen

Ross

Ross looked over his shoulder at the fertilizer spreader hitched to his tractor and breathed a sigh of relief. The relic was still operational despite its age and the rust coating its body. If he stayed and didn't sell out, next year or the year after he'd have to invest in a new one. But this one would do for another season, maybe two. By then he'd know what he wanted to do. More and more he was toying with the idea of leaving. As it stood, there was no real point in his staying.

Byron and Barbara Summerset were wasting their breath if they honestly thought Emma was going to change her mind, and living down the road from Miranda was becoming more painful as the days passed. Montana was looking more attractive by the hour. There would be support in Montana, a ready-made community of fellow strugglers looking for the same companionship and acceptance he wanted so desperately.

If leaving made him a quitter, so be it.

He drove the spreader down two more rows and was turning the tractor when an unfamiliar car came through the gate and barreled down the rutted drive toward the house. His eyes narrowed as he watched the car dodge the deepest holes and maneuver around the rough patches. Whoever was in the car knew the rutted path well. Miranda? Nah, she drove a Beetle, and after the things he said to her, she wouldn't come back here.

His mind raced. Not that many people came up the drive often enough to know it that well. Only him, and Miranda, and—

His mouth went dry and he watched the car bounce up the drive and pull up under the tree in the front.

That was where Emma parked.

He held his breath.

Nobody got out of the car for a minute, then his heart leapt to his throat as a girl got out. A girl with Emma's blonde hair and jaunty stride. Ross's breath turned into a gasp. *She's here.* Emma had come out to the ranch. Byron and Barbara must have convinced her to come out here and talk to him.

That didn't mean he was forgiven. Not by a long shot. But it was at least a start.

He killed the engine and left the tractor right where it was. He half jogged and half ran to the house with his heart in his throat. A part of him was elated and he wanted to gather her up and hug her until his heart stopped hurting. But he would wait to see what she said before he got too excited. For all he knew, she might have come out here to tell him to go to hell. He approached the house as Emma knocked on the door. Ross looked at her in horror. She didn't need to knock on the damned door. This was her home.

Though she might not feel that way about it any longer.

She knocked a second time, then pushed open the door and let herself in. He breathed a sigh of relief as he crossed the yard and followed her into the house. She was standing in the foyer and looking around uncertainly. "Nothing's changed," she said, more to herself than to him.

"No, I haven't changed anything," he said carefully. "It's pretty much the same as when your mother died."

She stepped into the living room. "I wondered if Miranda made changes. I guess she didn't."

"No, she didn't. We spent most of our time together at her place."

"I guess that makes sense." She looked at him with the same wariness with which he was regarding her.

"Make yourself at home. Can I get you anything?" *Which was stupid.* This was Emma's home. She should be heading for the kitchen without being invited.

"You have a soda?"

"Of course. Come on back."

She followed him to the kitchen. He handed her a soda and she sat at the breakfast bar on her old stool. He put a pod in the coffee maker.

"When did you start drinking that fancy stuff?" she asked as the coffee machine whined.

"When I sobered up. I needed something to replace the booze and the cook in Montana made it for all of us."

"Montana? Us? What are you talking about?"

"After I got out of rehab, I worked for nine months on a ranch in Montana that hires hard luck cases. Recovering alcoholics and addicts, PTSD soldiers, and such. We had access to daily AA meetings."

"Oh. I didn't realize you'd left."

"I guess Miranda never said anything. I was gone for over a year."

"She never told me you'd gone. She did say you had Covid. Was it bad?"

"Damned near killed me. That was when I decided to make a change. Take advantage of the second chance I'd been given."

"That's good." She took a big gulp of soda. "They told me. Pops and Babs. They told me about Mom and the men."

Ross shut his eyes and sighed. "*Damn.* Baby girl, I am so sorry. I never wanted you to know. If I'd known they were gonna tell you, I would have told them not to."

"They didn't want to. I guess they felt like it was the only way they could get me to come out here and talk to you. Besides, isn't it better if I know than for me to keep blaming you for everything?"

"I don't know." He got his coffee cup and sat on his stool. "You loved your mother so much. I didn't want that to be your memory of her. I wanted you to remember her as the woman we all thought she was."

"Everybody but Miranda. She knew the truth."

Ross's lips tightened. "And lied about it."

"She didn't want me to know. Just like you didn't want me to know."

"I blamed the theater and ran you off because of it."

Emma shot him a withering look. "Don't kid yourself. You did a lot more than be an asshole about the theater and you know it."

Ross winced. His daughter wasn't pulling her punches. "I do know, Emma. I drank like a fish most of the time you were growing up, and I neglected you and your mother. I missed your school programs and stuff at the church. I was a shitty father and a crap role model and I know it."

She looked at him shrewdly. "That's progress, I guess. That you'll admit it."

"I'd like to think so. Now I need to make amends for it."

"Part of AA?"

"A big part. We're supposed to make amends to everyone our drinking hurt. With your mother gone, you top the list. You grew up with a drunk for a father and that was wrong. So wrong." He took a deep breath. "We're to make amends whether or not the person we wronged ever forgives us. But you're my daughter and I have to ask. Is there any way, any way whatsoever, that you can ever see yourself forgiving me for all the stuff I pulled? For my part in the fiasco with your mother?" He felt tears welling in his eyes. "I love you, baby girl. I love you a lot."

"I see." Emma regarded him for a minute. "I have a question. You want my forgiveness for a whole hell of a lot. You're asking me for it. My question is, can you forgive Miranda for what she did? Can you forgive her for the lies she told?"

"No." Ross shook his head. "The lies she told are unforgiveable."

"Then why the hell should I forgive you?" Emma asked quietly. She set her soda can down and stood up.

"No, please. Please don't go. Listen to me, Emma." Ross stood in a panic. She was about to walk out of his door forever.

"No. You listen to me." She rounded on him with fire in her eyes. "Yes, she lied. She protected the woman who'd pulled her out of a hellhole and given her a second chance at life. She protected the girl she loves like a daughter. She protected a pair of clueless old folks who put their daughter on a pedestal, and she protected an iffy boozer who could have easily fallen off the wagon. My god. What a sinner. *Shame on her.*"

"She could have told me the truth," he said stubbornly, not ready to concede.

"So you could fall back in the bottle? You couldn't handle the truth."

He sank back onto the stool, his mind whirling. He was blowing this royally. "Sit down, Emma. Please."

“Fine. But you need to get down off your high horse about Miranda.”

“All right. I’m off my high horse. Maybe you have a point about what Miranda did. Why she told the lies she told. But what I don’t understand is why she didn’t tell me or someone else early on that Renee was cheating. Why didn’t she tell me or your grandparents? Or somebody?”

“Because Mom would have taken me and run.” *Run?* He gasped in horror. Emma looked at him with anguish in her eyes. “She had airplane tickets, Daddy. Tickets to Chicago that her boyfriend gave her. Mom told Miranda if she told you what Mom was doing, she’d use those tickets and take me to Chicago. She was about to go anyway. Even if you’d known where we were, you would’ve lost me.” She held up her thumb and her forefinger a half inch apart. “You came this close to losing me. Miranda was terrified. She believed Mom would’ve done it, taken me and gone. She decided the lies were better than risking that.”

Ross recoiled in horror at the thought. “My god. She never told me.”

“Did you give her a chance? Or were you a complete asshole?”

“No, I never gave her a chance. I should have at least talked to her. But I was so damn angry. And hurt. I found out in one fell swoop that both the women I loved had lied to me. It was a bit much.”

“You love Miranda?”

He nodded. “But that’s not worth shit without trust, and I don’t think I can ever trust her again.”

“More bullshit, Daddy.”

“Why is it bullshit? If she lied about that, she’ll lie about anything. Like your mother did.” He’d plead if he had to. “Can you understand that?”

“No, I can’t.” Emma shook her head. “You’re equating cheating on a husband to lying to protect somebody you love. Which isn’t the same at all. So let me ask you this. If Miranda had come to you and told you about Mom, or told you at some point when you were seeing her, would you have come to me and told me about it?”

“God, no. I wouldn’t have said a word. I would have done everything to make sure you didn’t find out.”

“Why? Why not run to me and tell me everything?”

"I never wanted you to know."

"Well, guess what, Daddy. *Neither did she.* She did exactly what you said you'd do. She lied about it. So I guess we need to add hypocrite to your list of sins."

Ross winced. "I never thought about it like that."

"You need to. You need to get over the 'She lied to me' bullshit and maybe think about why she lied and what you would've done under the same circumstances. Then you need to remind yourself I have a hell of a lot more to forgive you for than you have to forgive her for. Your sins are greater than hers ever thought about being."

Ross stared at his daughter. "So if I expect you to forgive me, I need to forgive Miranda."

"You need to do more than forgive her. You need to get your ass over to her place, beg her forgiveness and grovel until she says she'll take you back. Not because of me. I'll forgive you or I won't, regardless of what you do about Miranda. But because you and Miranda belong together."

His mouth fell open. "I thought you were pissed off we were together."

"I thought I was too. But I'm not. Daddy, Miranda's lonely. Life dealt her a shitty hand when her husband left and then Tommy died. She drank and had to go to rehab. Life dealt her another shitty hand when she fell for you and you kicked her to the curb. I love Miranda. She's been like a mother to me since Mom died. I want her to be happy. For whatever reason, it seems to be with you."

"I see."

"Besides, I'm not moving back. My life isn't on a farm anymore. It's in San Antonio. You'd be better off out here with her than without her."

Ross blinked and gave himself a minute to take that in. *She cared.* She might be angry with him and a long way from forgiving him for all the shit he'd pulled, but she cared enough about him to want him "better off" with Miranda. "You know, I think I'd be better off with her too."

"Then make it right with her."

Without giving him a chance to answer, she got up and left. A smile played around his lips as her car roared down the drive. *Out of the mouth of indignant daughters.* He needed to get his head on straight about Miranda. He needed to come to terms with why she was dishonest with him and get over it. He needed to plead for her forgiveness and do what it took to get back where she belongs. With him.

***

Miranda

Miranda stared down at the empty hamburger basket. “So. What do you think? As good as the burgers at her brother’s place?”

Emma swallowed the last bite of her fat cheeseburger. “Hmm. I think so. The ambiance isn’t quite as kitschy. Some people might like that. I like the kitsch.” They were eating at the new hamburger joint opened by the sister of a famous San Antonio restauranter known for his iconic burgers.

“I don’t miss it a bit.” Miranda polished off the last fry. “This one is situated where it’s gonna draw a different crowd, especially at lunch when time is limited.” The new restaurant was several miles from the original in a nondescript strip mall close to Fort Sam and several of the old money neighborhoods. Rachel had put them onto the place and Miranda shot off a quick text to thank her.

“How’s *Beauty and the Beast* coming?” Emma asked. The show was in the middle of tech week rehearsals and would open in two days, which explained their late evening dinner.

“Another winner if I do say so myself. Tammy’s finally figured out where to put her feet and the rest of it’s coming together wonderfully. You’re coming, right?”

“Opening night. I kind of wish I’d had time to do it. But my coursework calls my name. Loudly.”

“School has to come first. Are you squared away for spring?”

“Tuition paid. Courses chosen. I started to move into the dorms but got a load of the price tag and decided to stay with Pops and Babs since they don’t seem to mind my being there.”

Miranda smiled. “You know they’re good with it. Are you staying in the house or did you take over that nifty garage apartment where Kevin lived for a while?”

"Garage apartment. But I admit to eating with Pops and Babs when they're not at the lake." Emma's smile dimmed a little. "It's like eating Mom's cooking again."

"That makes sense," Miranda said. "Your grandmother taught your mom to cook. Maybe this summer Barbara can teach you to make a few of those wonderful dishes."

"I hope so." Emma looked at her cell phone and winced. "Uh oh, it's after ten and you have a long drive. I'm gonna shoo you out of here and send you home."

"I'll let you." Miranda fished out enough money to pay for both meals. "Don't argue," she said when Emma started to object. "You're a starving college student. Milk it for all it's worth."

Emma hugged her and they left the restaurant together.

The moon wouldn't rise until later in the night and the sky was dark but for the stars, which gradually brightened the farther she drove from the city lights. She rubbed her eyes as she pulled off the interstate and headed down the farm to market road. She was putting in unnecessarily long hours again this week, her sure-fire go-to rather than sit at home lonely thinking about Ross and what might have been.

She'd wondered if Emma wanted to talk about her father when she called earlier in the day and asked if Miranda was free for dinner. But Emma hadn't said a word about Ross, hadn't said whether she'd spoken to him or gone out to see him. Miranda had already decided to let Emma take the lead. She'd said her piece. It was now up to Emma what she chose to do. The girl was an adult now and capable of making the decision for herself.

Emma was an adult. That was a jarring thought. That meant that if Tommy had lived, he'd be grown by now.

She pulled into the ranch. Instead of driving straight to the house, she veered off and bounced down the drive leading to the cemetery. She used the flashlight on her phone to navigate to Tommy's grave and sat cross-legged on the warm grass where she could lean back against the headstone. "It hit me, Tommy. This evening with Emma. You'd be a young man by now. Making adult decisions. Making adult mistakes. I can't help but wonder what kind of man you'd have been."

She sat a minute and let the breeze play in her hair. "Emma's grown. She's an adult and I really can't tell her what to do any more.

She's still at odds with her father. Even now that she knows about her mom. I'm gonna have to let her make her own decision about that. But I hope she can forgive him."

She leaned back against the headstone and sighed. "I fell for him, Tommy. Her dad. But he found out I lied to him and he feels I betrayed him. He can't forgive me for it. Guess I don't blame him. I was trying to protect Emma, but he doesn't see it that way."

It was quiet in the cemetery like it always was. She hadn't come here this evening for answers. She'd come for the calm sitting here always gave her and was giving her tonight. She stayed a few more minutes, letting the peace and comfort seep into her heart, before dusting off her jeans and getting in the car. It was dark but for the stars splashing across the sky and she was almost to the house before she could make out the pickup truck parked in front and the man sitting on the front steps. At first she was alarmed, but as she drew closer she recognized the ramshackle old truck...and the man. Her heart started to pound like a drum.

Ross was here. Ross had come to her. It was the last thing she would've expected him to do, considering the way they'd parted. Her heart leapt and hope warred with wariness.

Why had he come? What did he want from her?

She pulled into her usual spot and walked slowly toward the house. She was almost to the steps when he stood. She tried to look at his face, to get a glimpse of his expression, but it was too dark to see anything. She stopped a few feet shy of the porch and looked at him in the shadows. "Ross."

He returned her gaze. "Miranda."

They stared at one another for a moment. He reached out his hand and she took it in hers. Together they sat down on the top step. "I'm sorry," they said in unison.

"Ross, I—"

"No. Let me go first," he said. "Miranda, I'm sorry I was such an ass and I'm sorry I took things so badly. I have no excuse except I lumped what you did in with what Renee did. Which was stupid. Cheating on me and trying to protect a young girl you love are two completely different things."

"I'm sorry, too. I know what I did hurt you. Maybe if I'd tried harder I could have come up with a better solution."

"I doubt it. You found yourself between a rock and a hard place. You wanted to protect Emma. First and foremost. I should have remembered that. I didn't."

"Maybe I should have called Renee's bluff and told you what was going on. Taken my chances with the airline tickets. Wait. You don't know—"

"Yeah, I do. Emma told me. Believe me, you did the right thing. If Renee said she'd use those tickets and run, she would have. It scares hell out of me to learn how close I came to losing my daughter. Really losing her, not just pissing her off."

Miranda turned to him in surprise. "Emma talked to you?"

Ross shifted on the steps. "Yeah, she came out last Sunday. We had a discussion of sorts."

"She didn't tell me. We had dinner together tonight and she didn't say a word." She glanced over at him. "Did the two of you make things right?"

"Not really." He laughed. "She let me know in no uncertain terms she wasn't happy with the way I treated you. Pointed out that I was a hypocrite. Said I needed to make things right with you. Threw the ball in my court so to speak and walked out. She wasn't all that diplomatic about it, either."

"Really? Sweet little Emma?" Miranda snickered a minute before sobering. "I trust there was more to the conversation."

"There was. She made me face a few hard truths. Like you did what you did to protect a lot of people, myself included, and I needed to remember that. And she pointed out if I'd known about her mother, I wouldn't have told her. I would've lied. Which is exactly what you did."

"Hence the charge of hypocrite."

"You got it." He dragged his hand through his hair. "She pointed out most adamantly I needed to forgive you."

"She did?"

"Actually, she said I needed to get my ass over here and grovel until I managed to make things right with you. Which I'm not doing a very good job of. I should have brought flowers or something."

"Nice thought, but not necessary. So she's okay with us as a couple?"

"Seems to be. She said you were lonely and life had dealt you a shitty hand and I seemed to make you happy."

"O-kay."

"Then she said she wasn't coming back here to live with me and I would be better off with you than without you. Kind of a backhanded way to say she cares, I guess. Even if she hasn't forgiven me."

"She will. Give her time to work through her issues. With the Summersets pushing for a reconciliation, she'll come around. She'll start to remember the dad you were before the booze took over." They sat in silence for a minute. "I should have tried harder with Renee," she blurted out. "I should've told her to get her butt home and try harder to make it work with you. Drag you to AA like she did me."

"I don't know if it would've done a bit of good. Anyway, what's past is past. I'm more worried about the present and where things go from here. Can you ever forgive me for being such a shit?"

"Of course I can. But can you ever forgive me for the lies I told?"

"Done and dusted."

"Are you sure?"

"Miranda, I love you. Forgiving you is part of loving you. And after Emma laid it out for me, I'm not sure you even need to be forgiven."

"You love me?"

"Sure do."

Miranda's heart about burst out of her chest. "I love you, too. So much."

He reached over and pulled her close. "Then let me kiss you. I've missed you. I've missed you so damned much."

"I've missed you too. I—" She gasped as his lips crashed down on hers. She clung to him, pouring a month's worth of loneliness and longing into the embrace. *Good, so good*, she thought as she opened her mouth and deepened the embrace.

She loved this man, who like a Phoenix came back from Covid and got himself sober. Against all odds, they'd found their way to one another. She wrapped her fingers around his neck and held him tight as she gave her heart to him. It was more than physical, this commitment they were making tonight. It encompassed their minds and their very souls as they acknowledged with their lips and their arms what their hearts already knew.

She could feel his love and his need for her as he held her close. Her body responded to his touch. But more importantly, her heart and her soul reached out across the chasm of loneliness and regret to embrace him as the man she wanted by her side.

They held on to one another for long minutes, kissing and touching and holding one another surrounded by the blanket of stars. When Ross raised his head, he whispered, "Damn, that was good. I could do a lot more of that given the chance."

"I could too."

Ross clung to her hand. "It's more like I need to. I need to touch you, to hold you close, to make love to you until we're both breathless. I need it way down deep."

"So do I," she said softly.

"But you want to know what I need the most?" She shook her head. "Waking up next to you. Reaching across the bed when we're both still half asleep and waking up with you in my arms."

"I miss breakfast," she said. "Drinking coffee with you while you tell me what you have planned for the day."

"Then it seems we have some mornings to make up for."

"We do."

They held hands in silence for a long moment. "How are we gonna do this?" he asked quietly. "You and me as a couple?"

Miranda squeezed his hand. "I love you and you love me. But we're not like a lot of other couples. We're recovering alcoholics. You're fairly early in recovery and I still have to deal with it every day. We need to take this slow and keep our relationship as stress-free as possible."

"How do we do that?"

"We spend time together. Date. Enjoy one another. Don't pressure ourselves. Let our relationship progress naturally. Don't rush anything. Give things a chance to grow."

"Is this gonna include some of those mornings and coffee?"

Miranda laughed softly. "You better believe it."

"Okay, then. Want to have one of those mornings tomorrow?"

"I would. I presume that means having the night together as well."

"You bet it does."

They held hands in the moonlight, neither seemed to be in a big hurry to start their night together. “I feel like I do when the Durango starts a new production,” she said.

“How’s that?” Ross looked at her curiously.

“Everything’s shiny and new. The possibilities are endless.”

“Huh, that pretty well describes it. It’s a new production for you and me. I can’t speak for you, but merely the thought of what wonderful things lie ahead for us is absolutely mind-boggling.”

Miranda had to agree.

Epilogue

Rachel looked over the sketches for the *Addams Family* sets, going over them one at a time. The outside of the mansion and the cemetery next to it were perfect. The derelict mansion loomed, rundown and spooky, and the fog-enshrouded tombstones painted on the back of the set added the perfect shiver. "You'd want to add dry ice fog from sources behind the fence," Harlan said, handing her a second picture, this one with an iron and stone fence in front of the painted tombstones. "That should give your actors plenty of room for whatever dance numbers are involved."

"I see," she murmured noncommittally. She loved the sketch, but she'd be damned if she let on. Especially to *him.*

Instead she nodded and picked up the next sketch, this one of the inside of the mansion. The walls of the mansion were the same painted-on stones as the outside of the house. Portraits of creepy Addams ancestors adorned the walls and wide pillars framed the front door at the back of the stage.

A sweep of stairs along one side led to a second level. A row of windows in the back looked out to leafless tree limbs and a shadowy full moon. "This wall does double duty." He pointed to the wall on the side. "With the stairs moved into place, the front door and windows can't be seen."

"Clever," she said more to herself than to him.

She flipped through the rest of the sketches. It killed her to admit it, but Harlan's ideas were wonderful. If he could translate the sketches into a set, they would have the perfect shabby, eerie, faded but elegant backdrop for the creepy but hilarious family they were bringing to life this winter. She handed the sketches back to Harlan. "They're good," she said grudgingly.

"Thanks," he said softly. His eyes met hers and held. *Damn.* She hadn't imagined the attraction in his eyes a few minutes ago.

He was as attracted to her, and she had to admit, she was to him.

This would not do. Not at all.

In fact, it made her angry that a man like him would be attracted to her.

That she would be attracted to a man like him.

Abruptly she shoved the sketches across the desk toward him. "The last performance of *Beauty and the Beast* is this coming Sunday. You can start building any time after."

His eyes widened at her unfriendly tone. Why he seemed surprised she didn't know. She'd made her feelings about him perfectly clear when Josh and Cameron insisted on hiring him. She might be forced to work with him but she'd be damned if she pretended to like it. And she'd be damned if she let the sexual attraction matter. It didn't matter if he was appealing, he was an ex-con, and not the kind of person who belonged at the Durango. Especially with all the children in the Academy. He wasn't the kind of man they needed to be exposed to.

"Fine. I'll do that." He gathered up the papers and stood up. He was halfway out the door before he turned around and faced her, his face a mask of stone. "Look, I know you don't like me and you don't want me here, but the powers that be overrode you and here I am, so the least you could do is be professional. I'm trying to be."

Rachel couldn't hold back. "They had no business hiring you, and I'll be damned if I put a happy face on it. I don't care if Miguel called in a favor. You're an ex-con. You have a history and a prison record. You cooked your goose when you broke the law."

He stepped back into her office and leaned over the desk. "So they had no business hiring me?"

"They have no business hiring an ex-con. Any ex-con. I don't care what you did or what you were in for. The law is the law and you broke it."

"Wow. I don't know why they bothered with a judge and jury." He sneered. "All they had to do was call you in and boom, it's all taken care of. You have no idea what I did or why. All you care about is I spent ten years behind bars."

"You got it." Her eyes narrowed. "Not that it matters, but what did they get you for? Drugs? Robbery? What did you do to get locked up for ten years?"

He leaned even closer, close enough she could feel his body heat and smell the mint gum in his mouth. "I killed a man," he said. "I went out and bought gun, and shot him in cold blood. Given the choice, I'd do the same thing again in a heartbeat."

He turned and left her office.

ABOUT THE AUTHOR

The author of over forty romance novels, Emily Mims combined her writing career with a career in public education until leaving the classroom to write full time. The mother of two sons, she and her husband split their time between central Texas, eastern Tennessee, and overseas visiting their kids and grandchildren. For relaxation Emily plays the piano, organ, dulcimer, and ukulele for two different performing groups, and even sings a little. She says, "I love to write romances because I believe in them. Romance happened to me and it can happen to any woman—if she'll just let it."

Connect with Emily:

facebook: emily.mims.756

twitter: @emilymimsauthor

instagram: @mims_emily

website: emilymims.com

www.BOROUGHSPUBLISHINGGROUP.com

If you enjoyed this book, please write a review. Our authors appreciate the feedback, and it helps future readers find books they love. We welcome your comments and invite you to send them to info@boroughspublishinggroup.com. Follow us on Facebook, Twitter and Instagram, and be sure to sign up for our newsletter for surprises and new releases from your favorite authors.

Are you an aspiring writer? Check out www.boroughspublishinggroup.com/submit and see if we can help you make your dreams come true.

Love podcasts? Enjoy ours at www.boroughspublishinggroup.com/podcast

www.ingramcontent.com/pod-product-compliance
Lightning Source LLC
LaVergne TN
LVHW090949080826
845145LV00003B/939

* 9 7 8 1 9 5 3 8 1 0 6 5 6 *